DADDY SYNDROME

JOYCE A. SMITH

www.jasmithproductions.com
@jawrites01

Book Design and Editing
Beyond the Book Media, LLC
www.beyondthebookmedia.com

ISBN: 978-1-953788-07-8

CONTENTS

SEASON TWO
My Black is a Weapon

SPECIAL THANKS

Author's Note: This was originally written in 2015. It took four additional years to finish this book for a total of approximately 19 years not counting the revisions. Since I first wrote these acknowledgments, many more people have played an instrumental role in my life. To my HTC family, thank you for the final push; your prayers and support were matchless. To Risha, Tashika, and the Brickhouse Suite (Elise, Philice, Tracey, Tinivia, and Courtney) thank you for your support and listening ear.

To my mother, Liz and my brother, Anthony, thank you for dreaming with me and for me when I couldn't see the vision for myself.

Finally, to my daughter Kailya, because of you, quitting was not an option.

ACKNOWLEDGMENTS

June 2, 2015

Wow, what a ride. As I sit here penning this, I can hardly contain my jubilance. It has been 7 years, and I am finally close to realizing the conclusion of a journey that started in the 8th grade with my reading teacher at Glasgow Middle School. She challenged us to write a creative story about Christmas. I remember the class laughing at my story, which would ordinarily be a good thing, except the story was a tragedy. I promised her I would dedicate my first book to her and here it is. I never thought it would be 20 years later, but here's to you, Mrs. S. Thanks for igniting the fire. I only hope there is a student out there for whom I have done the same.

Speaking of students, there are way too many to name, so I will do it this way: Smiley High School 1999-2000, Walterboro High School 2000-2001, Cohen High School and Sarah T. Reed, 2000-2005, Forest Brook/Smiley High School 2005-2008, and Dekaney High School- Thank you!

Thank you for the inspiration, the feedback, and the ear you provided as I spoke of my dreams. You guys have been my biggest cheerleaders and my most vocal critics.

To Sherelle (in my 7th period English class at Forest Brook) and Stephanie Rice from Forest Brook/Smiley, you two have been in my heart since day one. I can only hope that life has answered your dreams, and for the times you find it hard to dream and the moments you despair because you are not where you want to be, let me speak a word over your life. **Your past mistakes will no longer define you. You were created for a purpose and God loves you no matter what. He wants to use you and is waiting for you to return to his arms. Your life, the good and the bad, is what you make it. You have within the power to live victoriously. I BELIEVE IN YOU! You are worthy; you are special. You are loved. Any person or situation that does not please God or push you toward greatness has no room in your life. You deserve the best!**

I labored over this book and doubted myself for years. I tried to turn it into society's standard of a bestseller or great literary work. When I finally let go of man's expectations, things flowed. The impetus for this book is real people, embellished for enjoyment and peppered with events I experienced as a teacher. It's not pretty but neither are the lives these issues affect. It's gritty; it's faced-paced. I wrote it to spark awareness and provoke change. If you're looking for a book that will wax poetically, these pages are not for you. Pass it to the woman raising a daughter without a father. Pass it to the father who doubts his importance in his daughter's life. Pass it to the woman who has it together so she can be of aid to someone else. Buy a copy for the woman with a "baby mama" mentality who can't let go of her personal agenda and allow a good man to parent his child.

∼

The situations in this book are extreme but the devaluation of the human spirit is also real and comes on all levels; STOP THE CYCLE!

TONYA

DAY OF RECKONING

There are two kinds of people in this world. Those who make things happen and those who let things happen to them. I've always been a maker. I bet you knew I was going to say that, but it's true. I refuse to be a victim of circumstances or live a life that is less than what is inherently mine. I may not know why I was created, but obviously, it's for something great. Why would God put me in this body and give me this brain? Do I sound shallow? Trite, perhaps? Trust me; I am not exaggerating my abilities. I get stuff done. It didn't start out that way, but when my father divorced my mother, my daddy's little girl lifestyle went with him. I still made do. It took one time for the neighborhood skanks to tease me about my nappy hair and worn clothing and I started making my own money and stacking cash.

Two-parent homes were not that popular on my block, and that made me a target. My fifth ward neighborhood was a mixture of run-down houses and neatly manicured lawns. Corner stores were as plentiful as the winos who stood in front of them along with the candy lady, the basketball courts filled with dope boys and B-girls, plus the black and brown people just trying to make it.

When my daddy was around, I stayed fresh. He kept his baby girl looking tight, but if he hadn't put his foot down, my mom would have had me wrapped in clothes from head to toe, walking around Houston looking like a roasted peanut. The way I dressed, the jewelry I wore, and how I styled my hair was probably the only battle my daddy won. My momma would have been looking fresh too, but she was stuck on Holy like some people are stuck on stupid. I'll get to those types of people later.

Growing up, my momma ruled with an iron fist. She kept a clean house, cooked a fine meal, made sure we were at church on Sundays and could recite scriptures on demand. She stayed in the Bible so much, I wondered if she quoted Corinthians when he climbed on top of her *Love is patient, Love is kind.* I'm silly and wasting time. No point thinking about my parents. I haven't seen or spoken to them in years. My attention should be on my daughter Trixie. I knew she was causing trouble and not the usual teenage shenanigans. She needed an intervention, like a chair in front of the door while I waited with a belt in my hand. However, that wasn't my style. I'm not that girl. If I were my mother's daughter, I'd grab a Bible for guidance, but I refuse to touch one of those again.

TRIXIE

MIRROR IMAGE

T he scenery from the city bus passed by me in a blur. Occasionally, I'd glance at the old lady seated on the front row or imagine why the bus driver didn't shave off the bald spots scattered across the back of his head, but mostly I tried not to worry if my mother had already spoken to my principal. I was nervous. I knew my nervous observations and internal ramblings would not prepare me for the upcoming confrontation. If there was one rule Tonya Peterson enforced, it was academic responsibility. I was more afraid of the consequences I would receive for getting in trouble in my math class, than how my mother would react when she found out why I was always late.

"Hey, lil mama." I rolled my eyes and turned around to see a guy slumped down on the back row.

"What's a fine girl like you doing on this side of town?"

When I first got on the bus, I pretended he wasn't seated behind me trying to flirt, yet here he was pestering me again. It should have been obvious I was out of his league. My Gucci and his Polo from the outlet store were not going to meetup and live happily ever after. Unfortunately, for him, I wasn't in the mood to coddle anyone, "Meeting my pimp."

"It's like that? What I need?"

"Boy, please."

"Come on, girl. Stop playing. I got twenty."

"Now I know you tripping." I dropped my head and pretended to look at my phone.

"Say boo."

"Ugh, what? You're interrupting me."

"I can do thirty, or I'm off at the next stop," he said.

I glanced toward the front of the bus to make sure no one was paying attention then slid next to him and helped shimmy his pants down while palming his wallet in my hand.

"Help, help! He tryna get me."

I dashed towards the side door. He tried to follow me, but his pants kept him from running behind me. When the bus screeched to a halt, I pushed the back doors open and leaped from the bus. My feet hit the pavement scuffing my heels and challenging my balance. I threw one last look over my shoulder then ran around the corner. A few blocks away I took in the dirty streets and graffiti covered walls. Normally, I barely looked at this part of town the few times I caught the bus home. There was not a lot of black anything in my life. My neighborhood and my part of the school were mostly white kids or blacks like me, rich and far removed.

I leaned against the wall and rested my back on the black faces of George Floyd, Breonna Taylor, and Atatiana Jefferson. I knew those faces, most of the world did. Their murders shocked me out of my spoiled fantasyland. I was black. It could have been me.

***

The sixth grade was the first time I kissed a boy. I couldn't say what my motive was, but it was marginally pleasant, and he seemed to enjoy it. One afternoon behind the school building, I met Josh, a seventh grader who had the reputation of a troublemaker.

"I bet you think you all grown up, huh?" asked Josh.

"Look, don't make my boyfriend beat you up."

I walked a few feet away trying to quell my excitement at meeting my first older boy. Josh walked up to me, towering over me by at least a foot. He poked out his chest. I stared at the superman logo on the front of his shirt. He may have been tall, but his muscles had not developed.

"I ain't interested in your little bitty titties," he said.

"Well, watcha want?"

"I wanna touch something else."

"Like what?" I asked nervously.

"Your stuff."

"I don't think so," I walked away. Josh followed behind me then moved in front of me stopping my exit.

"So, you chicken? I knew you were still a baby."

A sense of uneasiness rumbled in my stomach. I knew the bad names teachers called the girls who hung around the older boys at school, but I couldn't quell my excitement.

"So, what you afraid of?" Josh asked, moving closer. I refused to be daunted, so I adjusted my shorts as he pulled me onto his lap. He started kissing my neck.

"I thought you didn't want to kiss me." He ignored me and tried to touch my private area.

"Stop, that feels weird. I'mma kick yo' ass."

His hand grazed the seat of my shorts. I hopped off his lap.

"Wait, Trixie, I'm sorry, I thought you knew how to do this."

"What! I ain't no hoe." I delivered several pops upside his head.

"Stop, girl, please," whined Josh.

I bet he was sorry he downgraded and hooked up with a sixth grader.

"Okay, but you just wait. I'm gonna tell," I said, adjusting my clothes.

"Who you gon tell? I could tell on you too."

"Well, we'll both get in trouble."

"They don't care about me. They been trying to get me outta here cause I'm too old. Anyway, you owe me."

I put my hands on the humps below my waist, "What you mean I owe you?"

"You can't get a man hot and not pay up," said Josh.

"I'm not giving you none," I said, rolling my neck.

"I don't want that. I want you to put your mouth on my thing."

"Ugh, that's nasty."

"No, it's not. Men love it."

"Does it hurt?"

"No. My brother says it breaks a body down. His girl gets everything she wants. Josh stared at me, excited at the prospect of his first time. It was in his eyes. I didn't fully recognize what that meant, but instinctually, I recognized it was big.

"Really, I won't get Ebola or something, will I?"

"You a girl, don't you know about that kind of stuff?" asked Josh.

"No, my momma freaks out if it even seems like I'm gonna ask her anything about sex." I sat next to Josh on the step.

"Mine too, I learned everything from my brother's porno tapes. He's seventeen, and his game is tight. So, you down or what?" asked Josh.

After that day, I was hooked. I felt important. Josh and I were a couple for about a month until he broke up with me for sharing our secret with another boy. At the end of my sixth-grade year, I had a resume of three boys and the knowledge that relationships cramped my style.

TONYA

PUFF PUFF WHIP-

I decided against waiting with a belt in the hallway and settled at the dining room table opposite the entrance. I wanted to fire one up, but I don't smoke. I don't need my temple defiled. My body, like my mind, was a weapon, always primed and ready. I exercised regularly, and I tried to eat right. I would have gone vegan, but everyone was trying it. I don't do bandwagons.

I glanced out the window and saw Trixie walking up the driveway. I rushed to arrange spreadsheets across the table to make it seem as if I were working. I didn't want her to think I was pressed. I played it cool when she entered.

"I don't want to hear a word, just go to your room."

"That's what I am trying to do." I crossed the open space and was in her face in five seconds flat. Her eyes widened slightly. I had never hit her, but apparently, she detected something in my eyes because she backed up a few steps as if those meaningless extra feet would stop me from opening a can of Sunnyside beat down on her.

"I was late for Mr. Denson's class because my cycle came, and the nurse was out today."

"Get to your room and stay there."

I knew she was lying. The message in my voicemail called it a "grave" matter. Trixie had not been tardy, had no absences, and until today, no disciplinary infractions. Plus her period was last week.

Trixie's room was not a typical teenage haven. Instead of posters and snapshots of friends hanging out together, high-end artwork adorned her walls like those placed throughout the rest of the house. Her furniture and accessories blended perfectly to present a mature look carefully crafted by my interior designer. I felt a moment of satisfaction as I looked around her room and at the pricey clothes arranged in her closet. *I did it.* I thought as I stared at the rows of shoes in her closet. There was no reason for her to behave so rashly; she had everything. All she had to do was earn good grades and stay out of trouble. Based on her recent behavior, I felt as if she spit all over my sacrifices.

"If I had one wish, you would be my boo, promise to love you," sang Trixie.

"Ray J is too fine. Man, if I had one wish, my wish would be to get out of this house, find me a sexy rapper, and lay up in our crib. I wouldn't have to clean, cook, or go to school. I'd be set," she mumbled.

"You'd be set alright, set for your dumb behind to get played. Turn that music off." I entered and sat on Trixie's bed.

"I don't feel like talking," said Trixie.

"Not my problem."

"You only want to talk when you feel like it."

"Look, I'm trying. What more do you want from me? I buy you everything; we go on trips-"

"Was the man I saw dropping you off last night your boyfriend?" asked Trixie.

"What were you doing awake to be in my business?" I asked.

"You never want to talk about what I think is important. I'm almost old enough to start dating. I'm simply curious about the men I see you with."

I flopped on the bed and spent a few minutes flipping through the fashion magazine Trixie had on her nightstand.

"Why don't you read teen magazines with black girls? Latinas?

"You find a high-fashion magazine with them on the cover let me know."

"Well, maybe I'll start one after I retire. Remember, you need at least four different-"

"It's always about money with you."

"Trixie, you need to focus on school so you can have a six-figure career. Money is power and influence. You can't depend on anyone to support you, not me, the government, and especially a man. I have the deed to this house and the title to the Audi parked in the driveway. I know you like the thug type, but that won't get you anywhere but dead, in jail, or on the street with all your belongings confiscated. That's why you need to stop messing up in school and drop the Ebonics."

"Is the white man I saw you with last night your boyfriend or your sugar daddy?" asked Trixie.

"Please, you've been reading too many trashy novels. Most of those men are just friends. Knowing influential people can get you entrance into all the right places. Have you seen a lot of men in this house?"

"No."

"That's because I'm very selective.

"But white men, momma?"

"Baby, I will deal with White, Asian, or Middle Eastern. The only color I see is green."

"That's not right."

I stared at Trixie for a moment, "No, what's not right is letting a man use you to get what he wants without getting anything in return. I'm going to make an appointment at the clinic to get you on the shot. Get a high-paying career, stack your money, then marry and have kids in that order. That way if he leaves you, you have skills and a full bank account."

I felt a tiny prickle of guilt at being so pessimistic. Still, I planned to make sure she could handle herself around the opposite sex.

"Momma, I'm still a virgin. I don't want to take birth control. I heard it makes you fat."

I tossed the magazine on the nightstand and examined my nails. Flawless as usual. I wished my natural nails would grow instead of wearing this fake stuff.

"This is not up for debate; we're going." I walked toward the door relieved Trixie appeared to be listening.

"So, what am I going to hear at school tomorrow?'

"This one guy got mad because I wasn't interested in him, and he ratted me out," said Trixie.

"Interested, huh? He ratted you out because you didn't like him. Sounds like a lie. You may wanna rethink what you just said. It's better if I hear it from you." I left the room with one last look in Trixie's direction and headed to my favorite chair. Those few minutes of mother-daughter chitchat had me feeling achy and jittery all at once. *Inhale. Exhale.* I closed my eyes and imagined Trixie and I in the mountains by the fire at our favorite cabin.

When I was a girl, my imagination became my salvation. After my parents separated and life got tougher, I created different fantasies-shopping on Fifth Avenue in New York, vacationing in Morocco, or white-water rafting with my husband and six kids. Yes, I always wanted a big family. Most of my childhood visualizations, I made a reality. Obviously, the husband part was out the window since some niggas just won't do right.

My cell phone buzzed, and Valerie's name flashed across the screen. Valerie was the true example of a ride or die. She's had my back against my enemies but called me out on my mess in private. She's been a better friend to me than I have to her, but we've made it work more than twenty years, so I must be doing at least one thing well.

"Yes, Valerie."

"No, ma'am. Why didn't you call me after you picked Trixie up from school?"

"Because I didn't pick her up. She caught the bus. No one told her to get in trouble."

"How many times do I have to tell you to spend more time with Trixie? Don't ignore the behavior. It only makes it worse. And another thing, you really need to let me recommend a good counselor."

"I already scheduled an appointment."

"Without letting me do the research! You need to make sure you and Trixie are seen by a qualified professional."

Valerie was the true definition of an elitist, but not in a good way. She wasn't concerned with labels, fancy cars, or Michelin rated restaurants. Instead, she was a credibility whore. The more prestigious the better. She'd spend ridiculous amounts of time reading reviews and fact checking certifications. One time she staked out a dentist's office to see how long the appointments lasted.

"He's as qualified as district personnel can be."

"A school counselor? They can't handle the stuff you have going on," Valerie said.

"You cannot psychoanalyze my daughter and me just because you almost have your doctorate degree. It will be fine; Trixie will be fine."

"Tonya, I think you're making the wrong decision. You

need a counselor to help resolve your dad leaving and the anger you have with Trixie's father. She needs a male figure in her life."

I had several curse words ready to roll off my tongue, but if I told her how I really felt-that a having a man around only added misery-she'd be at my doorstep ready to haul me to the nearest psych ward.

"The only reason I am not hanging the phone up in your face is because I respect our years of friendship. Never bring up my father, Trixie's father, or anyone else's father to me again. Instead, why don't you worry about why you can't make your husband a father with his cheating self."

The phone went dead. Valerie didn't deserve that, but she knew my past was taboo. She lived through the horror with me.

***

"I know what you did," fourteen-year-old Valerie Cunningham said as we walked home from school.

"You don't know nothing but the cupcakes you hide from your parents." I was not in the mood for more of Valerie's lectures. I don't know why she still tried to befriend me as poorly as I spoke to her.

"What you're doing is deflecting. I saw it on Oprah. You're taking the attention off you by pointing the finger at someone else."

"Don't you have something better to do than try to psychoanalyze me?"

Ever since Alicia and I had a fight, Valerie walked me home. I guess she thought she would hypnotize us out of fighting again.

"Nope, you're my first subject. You got lots of drama in your life. So, tell me, how you are dealing with-"

I turned towards Valerie and closed the distance between the two of us.

"For the last time, stay out of my business." We continued walking in silence until the yelling inside my house met us at the corner.

"So, this is it? You're just going to walk off and leave us?"

Through the front door, I saw my mother pointing her finger in my dad's face. My daddy's eyes were red and swollen. *"I'm leaving you. I will always be here for my daughter."*

"Let's go this way." Valerie pulled my arm, trying to steer me away from my house.

"Shush, come on." I led Valerie to the side of the house so we could spy on my parents through the window. From the outside, we could see them standing in the middle of the living room floor. My dad was gripping the handle of his suitcase, and my mom had her arms spread blocking the door.

"If you walk out of this door, Grant Peterson, don't come back for your daughter or me."

"Oh, so now it's manipulation? It's not enough that you want to be the man of the house."

"I have to be the man of the house because you couldn't handle the role while you were out drinking and hanging with your friends."

"At least I have friends. You ran all of yours away. Just like you ran me away. Tryna be so holy, dress down to your ankles, don't know how to laugh and enjoy life. You a cold woman in and outside the bed."

Valerie and I watched as my mom grabbed my dad by the neck of his shirt. They tussled for a few seconds until my dad pushed my mom onto the sofa. I held my breath, praying he didn't hit her. *"I'll be back to see my daughter."*

"You don't have one. There's nothing here for you anymore."

I raced to the front of the house to stop my dad from leaving. He walked by me without a word. I watched as he got into his 1987 Buick Regal and slammed the door.

We had the best car in Sunnyside. I loved riding with my dad through the neighborhood as we listened to music and I flexed on the girls in my block. Riding with my dad was special. Every Sunday we'd drive to River Oaks and look at the big houses. Sometimes we'd go as far as *the Woodlands. My daddy and I knew all the rich places. He said he was gonna buy a house for me and momma in one of those places one day. I knew he never would, but I loved that he loved me enough to dream. I'd buy one of those houses for my daddy when I finished college. To hell with my momma.*

The engine started and my heart dropped. I felt him leave. I gripped the door handle shaking it violently. He glanced at me sadly, briefly, then slowly backed out of the driveway. I held on tightly, my feet picking up speed as he continued to drive. I heard Valerie screaming in the distance, but I wouldn't let go. I couldn't. Abruptly, the car stopped. We stared at each other, my daddy and me, inseparable, until now. I let go. He drove. I never prayed for him to come home. God was dead.

SEASON ONE

THE EMPTY BUCKET

Trixie's high school was an imposing brick structure nestled among towering trees and manicured lawns. The building housed the general student body who took the basic state curriculum and the academy which was a preview to what one could expect at an Ivy League University. The demographics in the honor's academy were mostly white and privileged with a few splashes of color added since their parent's bank account overrode their skin color. And then there were the charity cases, at least that was how they were seen. I called them melanated potential, mostly people of color who were smart but underprivileged. They were fortunate to live right on the edge of the school zone and score high enough to enroll in the academy. I was not delusional. If given a chance, Trixie would be another black girl from a broken home. That's why I had to play hardball today. I hated going into battle blind, but I was more than prepared to bargain for a successful outcome.

"Excuse me. I have a 9:00 appointment with Mr. Tolliver. My name is Tonya Peterson."

"Concerning?"

"Tiffany Peterson."

"One moment, let me look up her name. Oh, ok. Yes, Trixie."

"That's correct." I knew I was laying it on thick, enunciating every syllable and adding crisp endings to each word, but Black people were always on the clock. No matter how much money and influence we amassed, the pressures of the skin we lived in were always present.

"Mr. Tolliver will be with you shortly. Please have a seat," said the secretary.

"I just don't understand why the staff and administration are white," I said as I settled into the waiting area next to Trixie.

"Mom, please," said Trixie, looking around for eavesdroppers.

"Well, it's the truth. Don't you think black people can run the school? Shouldn't the students see at least a few representations of their culture?"

"Yea, I guess so."

I took out my compact and reapplied a fresh coat of gloss. My face was flawless. Subtle hints of color with a dramatic eye completed today's look. I thought about adding a fresh layer of perfume but decide against it. They weren't ready.

"That's why you have to be ahead of the game. Your cute shape will not last forever; you've got to have a nest egg."

"Do you have a nest egg?" asked Trixie.

"Of course, I do."

"How much?"

"None of your business."

"But what if something happened to you?"

"I listed your name on all my paperwork. I have an attorney and an investment planner on retainer to guide you and your grandmother with protecting my assets.

"But I haven't seen my grandmother in years. What's that all about? I get birthday cards and phone calls, but I never see her or my grandfather.

A girl needs her mother. I didn't need mine, but a few times, I gave in and took Trixie to meet my mother at a neutral location. The visits barely lasted longer than an hour and were over if she brought up my father. After those visits, it felt good to see she was still alive and flourishing, but the anger and disappointment I felt at our severed relationship kept me from fully forgiving her.

"You just won't give it a rest. Your grandmother is an unforgiving hypocrite, and I don't want you around someone like that."

"But aren't I old enough to decide for myself?"

"You have a wonderful life. How many girls your age travel to the Poconos and the Bahamas for the holidays?"

"But-."

"Mrs. Peterson," interrupted the principal. "Step into my office, please. Trixie, wait outside."

I caught Mr. Tolliver, Trixie's principal, eyeing me in my white pantsuit as I started towards his office. In a blink, old Tonya kicked in as I brushed passed him.

"Trixie, with me, please."

"But I'd like the chance to speak with you about this delicate situation before I bring Trixie into the meeting."

I eye-balled Trixie and she entered behind me. I almost grabbed her by the back of the neck when she plopped into the enormous leather chair in front of Mr. Tolliver's desk. "Trixie stand up and wait to be seated," I said.

"No, please sit, both of you," said Mr. Tolliver sitting

behind his desk. I perched at the edge of my chair and crossed my ankles in my best debutant pose. I wanted him to see me as poised and feminine, everything his frumpy looking wife obviously lacked.

"Mr. Tolliver let me start by saying that abusive behavior, physical or otherwise, is not condoned in my household. Her father and I are well educated and work diligently to ensure that Trixie receives the best possible education. That is why this incident is so disturbing to us."

Mr. Tolliver shuffled through the papers on his desk to pull out Trixie's student folder.

"I'm glad we're working with the same understanding. I am also relieved there is a male presence in the home. However, it makes the situation I wish to discuss with you more disturbing."

"I'm afraid I don't understand."

I felt tension rest between my shoulder blades. I glanced at Trixie out the corner of my eye before I sized up Mr. Tolliver and decided my approach.

"There have been allegations-"

"Allegations or rumors?" I asked as Mr. Tolliver cleared his throat and shifted in his seat.

"There is a boy who stated he witnessed Trixie performing a sexual act on the side of the cafeteria," said Mr. Tolliver. A shiver of alarm ripple through my body.

"That's a lie," Trixie yelled.

"Quiet Trixie. And was this witness also involved?"

"No."

"So, let me get this straight. You have an eyewitness that saw my daughter performing a sexual act on her boyfriend?"

Mr. Tolliver shifted, "No, it was uh, several boys."

My stomach flipped upside down, "I apologize for my daughter's behavior. She and I have a strong relationship, and she spoke with me about what occurred. I've already arranged for her to attend counseling sessions in the afternoon."

"I'm glad you sought help for Trixie. I'll note that in her file," said Mr. Tolliver.

"Trixie, you can head back to class," I said.

Trixie stormed out of Mr. Tolliver's office with a look of disbelief. As natural as possible, I pulled my hair to the side to expose my neckline.

"Mr. Tolliver, I'd rather not have this incident on my daughter's record."

"But it's standard procedure to report such behavior," said Mr. Tolliver.

Standard procedure. Why are white folks always talking about rules and laws when they are the biggest scratch my back, take this bribe, group of people walking? He can save the bull for someone who hasn't played in his world successfully. Negotiation was always an option.

"Isn't it also standard practice to provide a safe and nurturing environment for the students here? Apparently, there was not adequate supervision for this to have occurred, and my daughter was bullied and tortured into fighting for her reputation."

"But you admitted-" stuttered Mr. Tolliver.

"I admitted nothing. I stated my daughter spoke to me about an incident that occurred on school property." I uncrossed my legs and leaned forward.

"Mrs. Peterson, you are blowing this out of proportion," said Mr. Tolliver shifting in his chair.

"I take my daughter's well-being seriously."

"I understand, but my hands are tied." An image of him tied and punished with a leather strap crossed my mind before I stood and walked to the corner of his desk. Maybe his wife wasn't as boring as she looked.

"What about Trixie being placed on in-school suspension

for yesterday's disturbance and her file reflects that she will seek professional help?"

"I can do that, but I don't feel good about leaving this off her record. What if something occurred again?" asked Mr. Tolliver standing.

I walked closer allowing my eyes to drift down his body and back up to his grey and white hair. Thick and slightly wavy, his hair was his best feature.

"Trixie won't have any additional incidents at school," I said as I pushed Mr. Tolliver into his chair and dropped to my knees. I knew he wouldn't protest. I watched him at most of the school functions last year. He spent a lot of time smiling and cracking jokes with the female teachers on staff while his wife flitted around, trying to look like a first lady.

"Mrs. Peterson, what are you doing?" asked Mr. Tolliver, scooting back in his chair.

"Sweetening the deal."

Five minutes later, I was in the visitor's restroom, and Mr. Tolliver was probably taking a much-needed catnap. I washed my hands and stared at my reflection in the mirror. For a second I saw the scared little girl I used to be after my daddy left. I stared her down until the new me emerged-a fierce woman who faced every battle with determination and always emerged the victor. My eyes, however, never changed. They told a different story.

Fall 1982

I raced down the street, determined to make it home before my endurance ran out and my luck ended. Every time my feet hit the pavement I cringed, positive my tormentors could hear my footsteps and labored breathing. I rounded the curb, and then stopped to dislodge a pebble from the sole of my left shoe. They were my favorite pair before they became my last pair of decent shoes. If decent was faded leather and crooked soles. In the months after my parents separated, my mother started tightening the purse strings and life changed dramatically. There were no more weekly hair appointments and spa pedicures. A few months ago my daddy would have replaced my worn Coach shoes with two equally expensive pair and the matching purse just to see me smile. Now, I'd be lucky to receive a new pair before my current ones were completely frayed.

Only a little to go. I didn't make it.

"Gotcha rich girl," taunted Alicia, one of my neighbors.

"I'm not a rich girl, and I wish you would leave me alone," I said trying to pass.

"Yes, your highness, whatever you say," said Alicia as a group of girls burst into laughter and trailed behind me jesting about my worn clothing and nappy hair.

They paid me back for all the times I snubbed them on the way to the exclusive private school my mother could no longer afford for me to attend. By the time I made it to my front door, I hated my father for abandoning me, and I hated my mother even more for pushing him away. I sat on my front steps, too drained to go inside to begin my long list of chores.

"Hey Tonya, come here for a sec."

It was Michael, an average-looking guy from the neighborhood. Like most of the boys in the area he spent time pursuing women and chasing stacks instead of getting a formal education.

"Go away. Don't you have some drugs to sell or something?"

"Why a black man gotta be a drug dealer just because he has fly gear and jewelry?"

"Please, I don't feel like being bothered."

"I got some money for you," he said.

"I ain't into selling drugs, so you better get away from here before my mother comes." I stood to go inside.

"It's not drugs. Just come and see what I got for you."

I trailed behind him to the back of my house where I learned first-hand the bargaining power a woman held. I was so immersed in my *tutelage I never noticed my mother witnessed the first of many trips I later took to the graveled alleyway adjacent to my house. In addition to the abrasions the rocks imprinted on my knees, I earned ten dollars for my time.*

I blinked rapidly in the mirror, but no tears fell. My stomach clenched in knots, and saliva filled my mouth. I raced to the trash by the bathroom door. Nothing. My stomach heaved, and again I waited, heart pounding in my ears. Nothing came up. I was empty.

EPISODE ONE

I AIN'T GOT NO DADDY

It's been a week since Trixie's conference with Mr. Peterson, and she and her mother were barely speaking. Trixie tried to get Tonya to share what happened after she left the principal's office, but she only said, "She fixed it." She also said she would break her jaw if she didn't find a new hobby, but Trixie knew that was fluff. Tonya was not a disciplinarian.

"Trixie, I need to speak with you a moment." Trixie looked up to see her math teacher Mr. Denson blocking the entrance to the room. Mr. Denson was a few years away from his tenth year of teaching when he got the job at McDuffie in the academy. To him, the opportunity to teach at a school where students excelled in academics and the parents were an email away was a dream job. However, he never expected spoiled and entitled kids embroiled in so much drama. Even though their parents were reachable at any moment, most of them wore blinders concerning their children.

"Yes, sir?"

"Uhm, considering the circumstances, I want you to move to the back of the class."

"I'm sorry I disrupted your class yesterday, but I can't have people disrespecting me."

"I'm not talking about yesterday, but your behavior in general," said Mr. Denson.

"What behavior?"

"Please take a seat towards the back of the room," said Mr. Denson walking into the room.

"But that's not fair. You can't do that. I'm calling my mother."

The intercom interrupted Mr. Denson. "Pardon me Mr. Denson, will you please send Tiffany Peterson to the counselor's office?"

"No problem. Trixie make sure you have your homework for tomorrow," said Mr. Denson trying to smile.

The counselor's suite was a real drab. The walls were puke green and divided by partitions. There was a conference room for parent meetings and the head counselor's office sat in the back corner. The school's clinic was in the same area.

"Are you Trixie Peterson?" asked the secretary.

"Yes."

"It'll be just a second. Why don't you have a seat, or you can look around."

Trixie wandered around the office looking at various posters on scholarship information, college enrollment, and test prep material. To the left of the nurse's door was a poster advertising services offered by a youth counselor at a local community center.

"Do you know anything about this community center?" asked Trixie pointing to a poster on the wall.

"Not really, but you can ask Mr. Clayton. He's ready for you."

Mr. Clayton's office was small and airless with pictures of students scattered over a fourth of the room. The smallest wall had religious relics and cheap quotes printed on card stock and framed. Numerous plaques and certificates acknowledging his years of dedicated service occupied the remaining space. McDuffie was his longest assignment. Before, he worked in five different districts in less than seven years. Each of those years, he won Rookie of the Year, Teacher of the Year, and Most Favorite Educator awards. Most of the girls at school thought Mr. Clayton was handsome with his shocking blond hair and muscular build. He was also a favorite among the staff.

"I asked your mother to come in earlier today so we could meet, and I could explain how these sessions work," said Mr. Clayton.

"I guess that's it for impartiality," said Trixie slouching in the corner.

"Not at all, I'm here for you. I told your mother that our sessions are confidential, and she has agreed to respect that. I assume you know why you are here?"

"Yea, my mom dimed me out and now I have to see you as a condition of my parole."

"Are you always this sarcastic?" asked Mr. Clayton, taking his office phone off the hook.

"Yep."

"I see. Well, let me repeat everything that occurs during our sessions is confidential. I won't say anything to anyone, including your parents."

"Everything is confidential?" Trixie asked.

"Yes. So, tell me something about yourself," asked Mr. Clayton, pulling out a notepad.

"I mean like what? I'm a little over five feet, and I have brown eyes."

"Let's not start with the obvious. Tell me about the incident that brought you to my office."

"Don't you already know that?" asked Trixie, determined to be difficult.

"No, I don't. I only know what a piece of paper reads; I want a firsthand account," said Mr. Clayton.

"I'm not ready to talk about that."

"Why don't you tell me about your nickname?"

"I've always been known as Trixie. In elementary school everyone called me by my real name, but after that, my nickname just stuck with me."

"Your parents call you Trixie too?"

"My mom does. My daddy ain't called my mom since the day he smashed so-"

"It's just you and your mom?"

"It's just me."

Mr. Clayton scribbled on his notepad then leaned back in his chair.

"I'm beginning to understand the root of your behavior. Girls without a father present-."

Mr. Clayton's secretary interrupted him over the intercom, "Mr. Clayton, we have a situation that requires your presence."

Mr. Clayton put his notepad inside his desk and pushed back his chair.

"I'll be right there. Trixie let's reschedule for next week. I'll walk you out the front door. I'm sure you'd rather head home than go back to math class for less than twenty minutes."

Trixie and Mr. Clayton left the counselor's suit chatting down the hall until they arrived at the front of the school.

"You normally catch the city bus home, right?" asked Mr. Clayton.

"Only when my mom is being petty," said Trixie walking out the school.

On the bus ride, Trixie had time to think and people watch. Her school was in a busy upscale area where there were not a lot of people strolling the streets unless they had a serious purpose and destination in mind. Looking out of the window, she imagined the small smattering of men on the sidewalk were business execs on the phone with their wives asking what was for dinner while hoping they wouldn't be sent to the store for a last-minute grocery run. The women dressed in designer spandex, were headed to playdates or meet ups with their girlfriends for a session of hot yoga followed by a skinny latte.

Eventually, the scenery and the people changed. The greenery grew stark or non-existent. Dilapidated, abandoned buildings littered the streets. Most of the people were alone, consumed with the need to get to their destination. Trixie wondered how many of these people knew their daddies. Realistically, she knew people from all walks of life experienced fatherlessness. Still, she felt like a hood chick from a HBO special. Think about it. Her mother had a college degree and a high paying career, but her dad wasn't there when her momma popped her out or brought her home from the hospital. Nor was he there to cringe and pretend his baby girl was not a budding woman the day she got her first period.

Trixie leaned against her front door and rummaged through her purse for her house key.

"Uhm, hey."

"Are you hungry baby? I cooked baked chicken, mustard greens, and hot water cornbread."

"So that's the strange smell-cooked food. I didn't know you knew what mustard greens were. Is that an apron you're wearing?" asked Trixie.

Tonya stood in the doorway with her hair pulled into a ponytail. She wore minimal makeup with a blue polka dot apron over her favorite pair of Ann Taylor slacks and blouse.

"Girl quit playing and go get washed up for dinner; you know we eat promptly at five."

"I thought we ate whenever takeout arrived."

Tonya leaned closer to Trixie, "You better watch your smart mouth. Now go do what I told you."

Trixie stumped off to her room, "I sure hope her ass ain't on drugs."

"Trixie, dinner is on the table," yelled Tonya. Trixie walked into the dining room to a fully stocked table.

"Mom, what's up with the Jesus music?" asked Trixie.

"It's gospel, and it's better than the derogatory music of the world." said Tonya as she swayed to the beat.

"Derogatory music of what? Did someone die?" asked Trixie, confused as she stared at the two men wearing clerical collars.

"Trixie Michelle Peterson, watch your mouth before these men of God."

"It's okay, I've had teenagers myself. I'm Pastor Donnelly, and this is Deacon Jackson. We're from Guiding Light Baptist Church. Trixie, you have an unusual name."

"Yes, I was in the world when I was pregnant," said Tonya.

"It's okay, Sister Tonya, we all fall short," said Pastor Donnelly.

"It's not my real name," said Trixie staring at Tonya.

"How was your day? asked Tonya.

"It was okay."

"And your counseling session?"

"Mom!"

"I already spoke to Pastor Donnelly, and he will be in agreement that you get the help you need," said Tonya gesturing for everyone to sit at the dinner table.

"You know Trixie, God is a God of chances, and no matter how many times we mess up, he's always there to pull us through. Isn't that right, Deacon Jackson?" Deacon Jackson nodded his head, keeping his good eye on Tonya as Pastor Donnelly blessed the food.

"I think it is wonderful that you're seeing a counselor," said Pastor Donnelly helping himself to a spoonful of greens.

"I guess, but I'm not going back," said Trixie.

"The hell? Excuse me, pastor," said Tonya, squeezing Trixie's knee under the table.

"Trixie, why don't you want to continue your sessions?" asked Pastor Donnelly.

"Thanks for asking pastor, I don't like Mr. Clayton."

"Well honey, that's just too bad. You deal with all sorts of people in life. Mr. Clayton seemed perfectly respectful to me," said Tonya.

"And you know this because of your keen parental instincts, right mom?"

Tonya took a big gulp of tea and glanced at Pastor Donnelly from under her lashes. Pastor Donnelly was what many called a pretty boy. He had light eyes and a slender build. In his twenties, people labeled him as a man-whore or gay. After he accepted the call to ministry, it was hard to find a church to hire him as pastor since most of the congregants thought his presence guaranteed a bevy of women fawning over him every Sunday.

"Actually, I think it's important Trixie has a rapport with her counselor. I'd be happy to speak with you. I have a degree in pastoral counseling, so I'm sure your principal won't mind," said Pastor Donnelly.

"Thank you, pastor, but that won't be necessary," said Tonya.

"I know someone. Her name is Awana Thompson, and she works at the 3rd Ward Community Center."

"I know that place. It has an excellent reputation," said Pastor Donnelly.

"Yep, I have two foster children she counsels. They love her," said Deacon Jackson, breaking away from his meal long enough to chime in.

"Give me the information, but I'm not so sure about the area where she works," said Tonya.

"Didn't you grow up there?" asked Trixie.

"That was years ago, and things have changed. I said we'll see." The small dinner party lapsed into a comfortable silence as they grubbed on Tonya's home cooking.

"Well, Sister Peterson, it was nice fellowshipping with you and Trixie. However, I must be moving along. I have a church member in the hospital I need to visit," said Pastor Donnelly.

"Can it wait until after dessert? I baked a cake from scratch," asked Tonya.

Pastor Donnelly put his hands on his hips, and struck a funny pose, "No sweets for me, I'm tryna watch my figure."

"Oh pastor, you're so funny," said Tonya leaning towards him.

"See you at church Sunday, Sis. Peterson," said Deacon Jackson blocking Pastor Donnelly from Tonya's view.

Tonya stood at the door watching them walk to the car. In the dining room, Trixie sat at the table in shock. A part of her prayed Pastor Donnelly wasn't her mom's future sugar daddy, but Trixie also wanted him to stick around and have a positive effect on her.

"Whew, the way she was looking, you would have thought you were the dessert," joked Deacon Jackson as he walked down the driveway.

"I saw you giving me the side-eye while you were stuffing

your face. Tell me what you think," said Pastor Donnelly as they entered the car.

Tonya slammed the front door and marched into the living room, "What the hell did you do to Mr. Clayton?"

Showtimes over thought, Trixie. "Nothing. He just seemed creepy."

"Creepier than the boys you were messing with at school? Thought not. You will continue your sessions. Period."

Trixie turned away from Tonya and rolled her eyes, "How did you get those preachers over here? Preachers don't show up at strange women's houses."

"All churches speak one language, and it ain't tongues. It's money, and I have plenty of it," said Tonya grabbing a piece of ice out of her glass.

"How are you going to hook a preacher, and we don't even go to church," Trixie asked, bringing the dinner plates into the kitchen.

"That's okay; we'll be there Sunday."

"Nope, not me. I ain't got no daddy, and I don't need one."

"I'm glad you've moved on from worrying about your sperm donor. You cannot make people love you. The sooner you understand that the better. Pastor Donnelly will make a good role model. You need someone to guide you around all the games little boys your age like to play."

"Lucky me," mumbled Trixie, rinsing a plate and placing it in the dishwasher.

"Excuse me?"

"Nothing."

EPISODE TWO

FINE AS WINE

Years ago, The Galleria mall provided an impressive shopping experience for the discriminating buyer. Now, outside of a few high-end stores, it was the place to be seen by wanna be ballers and clout chasers. Tonya preferred Market Street in the Woodlands, but that crowd was too lame for Trixie's taste, so she convinced her they could find everything in the Galleria area.

"You can't wear that to church," said Tonya as she shuffled through the racks at Neiman Marcus.

"But mom, it's cute."

"Yea, for a hooker on the prowl."

"But isn't that the point?" Trixie asked, placing the burgundy dress back on the clothing rack.

"Yes, but don't let the world know it. Some women dress for the occasion, smart women dress for the man."

"I get it; old preacher equals mumu looking dress."

"No, smarty pants, you still have to be in high style, just understated."

"Oh," Trixie said, moving to the sales rack.

"Look, you're old enough to shop for yourself; let's meet at the food court in two hours."

"Can't we shop together?"

"Trixie, two fifty is your limit," said Tonya, handing Trixie her American Express card.

Trixie had mixed emotions about shopping without Tonya. Clothes were the only topic they had in common. Sometimes Trixie tried to select the most outlandish outfit just to spark an argument or have Tonya explain the rules of engagement, which, according to her, were simple. First, a successful business owner knew her audience and the tone she was trying to set. For instance, about a month ago, Tonya was attempting to close the deal on a six-figure investment. Instead of wearing the traditional navy or black suit. She wore cream and red. The cream color was classic and refined, while the red accents provided just enough boldness to show her clients that she would grow their portfolio with the right blend of risk and research.

Trixie loved the moments when Tonya shared business tips with her or asked her opinion on certain business situations. While Trixie didn't understand most of Tonya's job, she had a head for business. Her goal was to be a savvy business owner or a corporate attorney who handled mergers for overseas clients.

Not in the mood for shopping, Trixie headed to the jewelry store. Jewelry was another fashion statement Tonya and Trixie had in common. Tonya already had an impressive collection she would pass to Trixie when she married, but Trixie was eager to start a collection of her own. She stood admiring a pair of diamond studs when she heard a deep voice over her shoulder.

"Beautiful, aren't they? Hi, I'm Bryan." Trixie turned towards Bryan, ready to put him in check.

Damn, he fine. Hey, future baby daddy. Trixie smiled slightly and slid further down the display case, checking out his biceps as she went.

"Excuse me. I would like to purchase these earrings. Also, let me have the matching bracelet," said Bryan, placing the items Trixie had been admiring on the counter.

"Must be a very special lady," said the salesclerk.

"We'll see," he replied, pulling out his wallet.

Trixie didn't realize she was staring until he winked at her before heading out the store with his purchase. Deflated, Trixie left the jewelry store to start shopping. With thirty minutes to spare, she found a dress Tonya would like then headed to the food court. She settled at a table and pulled up her favorite playlist.

"You know you should try listening to jazz," said Bryan over her shoulder.

"Please, that's for old folks," Trixie said, not looking up from the screen.

"Do I look old to you?"

"Not really."

"Good, I'm only twenty-two. Are you a college student?" said Bryan.

"Yea."

"I saw you admiring those earrings a while ago," said Bryan, sitting next to Trixie.

"I can't afford them."

"I remember my broke college days. What's your major?" asked Bryan.

"Psychology," Trixie lied.

"I studied music. Let me introduce you to a few of my favorite Jazz artists," said Bryan, pulling out his phone.

***

Trixie lay sprawled across the bed, admiring her new bra

and panty set. She switched her cell to speaker mode then arched her back off the bed, staring at her figure in the mirror.

"No, I don't have a boyfriend."

"That's hard to believe. A pretty girl like you on a college campus, I know the boys hit on you all the time," Bryan said.

"Not really."

"I guess that's to my benefit."

"Tell me why you put the earrings in my bag."

"A beautiful gift for a beautiful girl."

"But they cost so much," said Trixie with a grin.

"Don't you know you're worth it?" asked Bryan.

"If you say so."

"When can I see you again?"

Trixie got off the bed and walked into her closet, "I'm not too young for you?"

"No. Let me take you to dinner tomorrow night."

"We just met."

"You're not going to turn down the man who bought you those earrings, are you?"

Inside the closet, Trixie pulled out a pair of heels, dark skinny jeans, and then rummaged through the shelves looking for her red crop top.

"Okay, what time?"

"Eight o'clock." Outside her door, Trixie heard Tonya walking down the hall.

"Look, I gotta go. I'll call you tomorrow," Trixie said as Tonya entered her room.

"Trixie, didn't you hear me calling you?"

"Sorry, I was half-sleep."

"Let me see the dress you purchased." Trixie pulled out a medium length white dress with blue flowers. It had a matching jacket to cover the spaghetti-strapped sleeves.

"This is cute," said Tonya sitting Indian style on the bed.

"What type of jewelry should I wear?" asked Trixie.

"Something understated to match the style of your dress. Do you have something?"

"I think so. Momma, you ever slept with a man for something like jewelry or a nice outfit?"

Tonya moved to place Trixie's dress in the closet, "What kind of question is that?"

"I was just wondering. What if a guy bought you nice jewelry? Would you do something as a thank you?"

Tonya squeezed Trixie's shoulder on the way out the door, "I worked hard to ensure you never have to do those things. That's what you need to remember. Good night."

After Tonya left, Trixie turned off the lights and crawled into bed. Bryan was different. He was sophisticated and talking to him was easy. Trixie hoped he liked her enough to stick around.

I'm better at finding a nice guy than my mom, Trixie thought as she brushed the jewelry box hidden under her pillow.

Mr. Clayton, handed Trixie some of his chips, "Okay continue."

"It's a waste of time. Most of the teachers don't want to be here, anyway. They give us an assignment, and then they sit at the computer all day."

To Mr. Clayton, Trixie was like all the other girls who came in his office: fast and according to them, blameless. He was sick of kids who always pointed the finger at the system. Mr. Clayton took a sip of water, "How does that make you feel?"

"Unimportant."

"Well, you're in the magnet program, and we expect the students here to be autonomous, that means…"

"I know what it means," said Trixie, rolling her eyes.

Trixie stood up and walked the few feet of space in Mr. Clayton's office. She opened and closed her fist repeatedly.

"I don't need help with my schoolwork, but it still feels good to have someone concerned about if I understand. I thought teachers are supposed to care about their students."

"I know that wasn't easy to admit. Thank you for sharing.

Who are the people that care the most about you?" asked Mr. Clayton, scribbling notes.

"Well, Mrs. Brewster, my English, is patient. She always comes to work and attends school activities."

"Good, who else?"

"Some of my male associates care about me."

"Do they?" asked Mr. Clayton.

"It would upset them if something happened to me."

"So, to you, a part of caring is actively showing concern. Anyone else?"

"Well, I would say my mother, but I'd be stretching it a bit."

Mr. Clayton leaned forward. "How so?"

"Well, she cares about what I do, but only because if I fail, she looks bad. That's not genuine," said Trixie.

"So, Mrs. Brewster and your male admirers want nothing from you. Their concern is unconditional."

"No doubt."

"Trixie, it seems as if your logic is off a bit. I'd like to help you understand some of your faulty reasoning if that's okay."

"I guess, but I reserve the right to not answer."

"Fine, have a seat, please." Trixie sat across from Mr. Clayton, who had adjusted his chair for maximum contact.

"Now Trixie, what I've heard you say for the past few minutes is that someone needs to be genuine with you, is that correct?"

"Uh, huh."

"You mentioned Mrs. Brewster and how she shows she cares for her students. What if all of her caring comes from the need to keep her job or get a big fat raise when her students pass their exams?"

"Whatever," said Trixies.

"Just think about it, she's nice, she comes to work, and

the students love to be in her class, so naturally they perform their best. That could be artificial."

"It's not like that, you don't understand."

"What about your male friends? Do they care about you because they would miss you if you're not around? Don't they have something to gain if you're present at school?" said Mr. Clayton.

"But it's different with Mrs. Brewster."

"And the boys?"

"Well, I don't know what I get from their attention. It kind of seems one-sided, but that doesn't mean they don't care," said Trixie.

"So, you have two people in your life that you believe care about you, even though one of those relationships is in your own words, one-sided. What about your mom?"

"She just wants me to do well so I can get into a good college, and she can brag about me to people. That's artificial, too," said Trixie.

"Right, I understand, she pushes you to achieve, and as a result, you excel and become successful in life. What reward does she deserve for her hard work?" asked Mr. Clayton.

"You mean since she can't get a big fat paycheck from the district?" asked Trixie evading the question.

"If she could, I'd be out of a job," joked Mr. Clayton.

"Well, I guess our session is over," said Trixie walking towards the door.

"That works. I'm taking off early to meet my girlfriend."

"Is that why you're looking extra fancy today?"

"You like?" asked Mr. Clayton, popping his lapels.

"You cute or whatnot," said Trixie.

Mr. Clayton placed an arm around Trixie's shoulder and walked her to the door.

"You did super today, Trixie. See you next week?"

"I'll be here."

Mel's diner was a quaint, out of the way spot known for its greasy burgers and buttermilk flapjacks. The tastiness of the food was questionable since its late hours made it popular with clubbers and weed heads. Still, during brunch, the diner saw a steady flow of customers who usually purchased off the breakfast menu. I leaned back and watched Valerie's car slide into a parking spot at the far end of the building. She stepped out the car in a pair of cute Alexander Wang booties, a tailored pencil skirt, and a flesh-colored blouse. She was bringing the drama.

"I expected you to be here but not binging on a double stack of pancakes. Bacon too? You really are dealing with some things," said Valerie.

"Bacon and Keto are best buds."

"At least someone has a best friend,"

said Valerie, sliding into the booth. I cut into my stack of pancakes and slid half of them across the table.

"Did you come here to get on my nerves or to say you're sorry? You look cute."

Valerie rested her elbows on the table and propped her head.

"Thanks, I went shopping online and started buying colors other than black. I'm trying to better myself, I guess. I had my first counseling session yesterday."

I poured syrup on my pancakes then pushed the bottle towards Valerie.

"I'm trying to cut down on my sugar intake. I'll just use butter," said Valerie, eyeing the syrup bottle.

"Don't let Pierce make you doubt yourself. Who eats dry ass pancakes? There is nothing wrong with you. If your self-esteem needs a boost, we can work out and get your body snatched. I cannot stand him. I always had a terrible feeling about him. It's his name, with his high yellow self."

"You are the last person to call anyone pretentious. Look at you. You always look like a celebrity. You are the only person I know who comes to a hole in the wall to eat pancakes in a custom outfit," said Valerie.

"I've been wearing custom clothes since high school. They might have been knock-offs, but no one could tell the difference."

"I remember how good your sewing skills were. We were always the best dressed during homecoming week. My prom dress is still in my closet."

"Mine too. I can fit into my dress. You need to donate yours."

"Ha ha, jokes."

Valerie grabbed the last strip of bacon and handed me half. She took slow, exaggerated chews while I glared at her over a glass of juice. The server, Lou, strolled over with a look of irritation.

"Are you ordering or munching off your friend's plate?"

"Are you going to stop dying your hair with box color

and wearing clothes three sizes too small?" I asked as Lou scuttled back behind the counter.

"You called that one. Her roots need a serious intervention," said Valerie.

"Have you gotten over yourself yet? I need to know so I can unblock your number."

Valerie gathered her purse and started sliding out the booth.

"You can keep it blocked. I'm sick of kissing up to everybody and sugarcoating the truth. 'Watch what you say, Valerie, moderate your tone.' I'm always tiptoeing around Negros and their feelings. If I speak up at work, I'm a sista with an attitude. You're my friend. I should be able to-"

"Please stop. No one told you to keep quiet or make stuff all pretty. Just spit it out."

"I saw your mother yesterday." I shoved my plate to the side and piled my used napkins on top.

"I'll talk to you later."

"Please Tonya, wait a minute. I only went to get your dad's information."

"That is not your place. He is my father, and I'm too old for punishment. My mother is a mean and hateful woman. I don't want her in my business or my life, and you know this."

"I'm sorry, but I'm worried about Trixie, both of you."

"I'm fine. My daughter is fine. I do not need you messing around in my life trying to reconcile my father and me. He should have thought about that before he left."

"He didn't just leave; your mother ran him away."

"Look, I don't know what you're trying to prove. However, if all you want to do is stroll down memory lane, you can do it without me."

Valerie grabbed my hand and pulled me back into the booth.

"Pierce has been cheating on me for a year. I guess she

must be someone special. They met at the gym. She's one of those Vegan eating, almond flour using, embrace your natural, no butt kind of chick. The exact opposite of me."

"Right because those hips say fried pork chops and cornbread."

Valerie smoothed her hands down the sides of her pencil skirt, "Why do you always have to make fun of my weight?"

"Bump your weight. Where does she live and what type of car does she drive?"

"They have humiliated me enough. I am not about to do a drive-by like a hood rat." Valerie fished inside her purse, pulling out a twenty-dollar bill.

I pocketed Valerie's money and grabbed my purse, "I'm sorry I keep sticking my nose in your business."

"Stop being dramatic. Just get the information. You know I don't fight with my hands."

EPISODE FIVE

TIPPING POINT

Carol's Restaurant on the North side was the perfect spot for Bryan and Trixie. It was far enough from Trixie's side of town that she didn't have to fear being spotted, yet elegant enough to make her feel like a grown-up. Soft music played throughout as a fire glowed between a metal grate.

"How's your pasta?" asked Bryan.

"Divine," said Trixie, dabbing with her napkin.

"You are so mature for your age; I know you've been to better restaurants before, but-"

"No, this is great. My mom doesn't cook much, and I can't boil water."

"I'll teach you how to cook," said Bryan, leaning over the table to feed Trixie a breadstick.

"You will?" asked Trixie, trying to figure out how that would work.

"Sure, every girl needs to know how to cook to please her man."

"You can cook?"

"Yes, when I was growing up, my parents were never

around much. I guess they thought buying me everything would make up for their absence."

"That must have been hard. At least I never had a father to miss," said Trixie.

"It probably feels the same. But enough of the dreary stuff, tell me about you?"

For the next hour, Trixie and Bryan fed each other spoons of Tiramisu and traded stories. Trixie was so relaxed and in awe of Bryan, she felt like she was floating.

"How about after-hour drinks at my place? I make a killer virgin daiquiri," said Bryan.

"It's almost my bedtime," said Trixie.

"Come on, loosen up. Let's go for a walk. I know the perfect spot."

"I guess I can study for my class later. I do have an 'A' in it," preened Trixie.

"That's my girl."

The walk was perfect. The company was excellent. The entire night was perfect; so perfect that Trixie did not arrive home until 2:30 in the morning. Parked several doors away from her house, she and Bryan relaxed and listened to his latest playlist for another hour.

"This is nice. I can't believe how much I like Jazz," said Trixie.

"Have you listened to the music I bought you?"

"I listen to it all the time. It relaxes me. Man, I can't believe I stayed out this late."

"Yea, the time passed." Lulled by the electrifying sounds of Cassandra Wilson and the night sky, Trixie leaned in and softly kissed Bryan on the lips.

"Uhm, that was nice. I hate for tonight to end, but it's late," said Bryan.

"I guess I should be going."

"Maybe you can come to church with me one Sunday. I think you'll like it."

"We'll see," said Trixie, reaching for the car handle.

***

The next few weeks for Trixie were amazing. She spent hours video chatting with Bryan, her mom went back to her own world, and her sessions with Mr. Clayton were going well. His sunny personality and genuine desire to help put Trixie at ease. Eventually, Trixie shared how scary it felt to grow up without a dad. Mr. Clayton also helped her release some of the anger she felt toward herself. The day of her last session, Trixie was nervous because Mr. Clayton told her they would deal with her self-destructive behavior.

"So, tell me about your relationship with your mother," asked Mr. Clayton.

"What relationship? She's hardly around unless I do something to embarrass her."

"How does that make you feel?" asked Mr. Clayton.

"Just great, what teenager wouldn't love to have a mom who doesn't give a damn?" asked Trixie with a giggle.

"You say that jokingly, yet I can sense the pain in your words. Tell me about your father." Trixie leaned forward and placed her elbows on her thighs.

"Don't know him."

"You mean you do not have any idea who your father is?"

"Nothing but a first name, but you wouldn't know about a one-parent household, being white, I mean."

"You're right, my father was a constant figure in my life, but sometimes that's not always a good thing."

Mr. Clayton moved closer and handed Trixie a tissue. "What about a father figure?"

"Does Dr. Phil count?" quipped Trixie.

"That explains a lot of things," said Mr. Clayton.

"Like what?"

"Well, for starters, you use the time you spend with young boys to replace the lack of relationship you have with your father."

"That's crazy. My father is the last thing on my mind," said Trixie, disgusted.

"I don't mean in a physical sense. Fathers should make their daughter feel beautiful and protected."

"I don't know about all of that stuff. I don't need anyone to protect me."

"Yes, you do. All young girls do. I can help you if you just let me," said Mr. Clayton, sliding his rolling chair around his desk. Trixie didn't notice how close Mr. Clayton had gotten until he put his hand on her shoulder.

"Do you want help?"

"Yes," said Trixie earnestly.

"Tell me what you do to them," Mr. Clayton asked, sliding lower in his chair.

"Huh?"

"When did you start experimenting?" asked Mr. Clayton.

"During middle school."

"Did you let them touch you down there? Did you put their thing deep in your mouth?" Mr. Clayton moved closer and twirled a strand of Trixie's hair with his finger.

Man, this guy is tripping. He should know not to put his fingers in a black girl's hair.

Trixie's thoughts raced and crashed as Mr. Clayton fondled her hair, "Mr. Clayton, I think I should go," said Trixie.

Trixie tried to leave, but Mr. Clayton shoved her face in his crotch, grinding so hard she could barely breathe.

"Don't go, Trixie. Let me help you. Show me how you do it," said Mr. Clayton.

Trixie struggled to getaway. She could feel his hardness through his pants.

"That's it. Everything will be alri- Ah Ah, Ohhhhhh!"

Mr. Clayton snorted and squirmed so much Trixie was afraid he was having an asthma attack. For the first time since she started experimenting with boys, she was afraid.

"You okay, sweetie?" Mr. Clayton released Trixie and grabbed a few tissues to wipe inside his pants.

"Yes, sir," said Trixie, trembling.

"I think this session went very well, but I think we need to meet a few more times. For our next session, we will delve deeper and try to resolve the anger you have towards your mother," said Mr. Clayton as he straightened his clothes and resumed a professional posture.

"Okay."

"Remember, everything is confidential in our sessions. It's common to feel certain emotions after a therapeutic session like this one. If you have any problems, please call me," said Mr. Clayton, handing Trixie a post-it with his home and cell number written on it.

"Okay," Trixie repeated.

"See you next week."

***

Trixie burrowed under a pile of blankets while the alarm blared from the nightstand. One poorly manicured hand snaked towards her cell phone, silencing the noise. She'd spent the last few days hiding in her room trying to avoid Tonya's questions about Mr. Clayton. She still needed to process if what happened in his office was her fault. Maybe her reputation had influenced him.

"Uhm," moaned Trixie attempting to get from under the covers. She propped half of her back against the headboard before Tonya burst into the room.

"I can't believe you're sleeping under clean sheets with the clothes you had on yesterday," said Tonya tripping over a pile of clothes. Are you pregnant?"

"No, I told you I'm still a virgin. I've just been feeling achy."

"Well, get unsick because you are going to school on Monday. I called the school, and your teachers emailed the work you've missed the last two days," Tonya said, turning to leave.

"Momma, can I talk to you," Trixie asked, getting up to strip the sheets off her bed.

"We can talk in the car. I don't want to be late, and when we get back, clean this room," said Tonya leaving.

"Wait!" said Trixie in desperation.

"What is it?"

"Can I go to counseling at the youth center, please?"

"Look, I don't have time for this discussion," said Tonya heading out the door.

"Momma, would you just listen to me," cried Trixie wiping at tears.

"What did you do this time?" asked Tonya. Trixie slumped on her bed.

"I didn't do anything."

"Listen, Trixie, you need to stop messing up your life. You can't get into a good college with this foolishness."

"Is that all you care about!"

"I invested a lot into you, Trixie. The least you can do is go to college and become self-sufficient. When you have children of your own, you'll understand."

EPISODE SIX

#STUCKONSTUPID

Guiding Light Baptist Church was one of the largest churches in the city. It was only 8:15, but the parking lot was more than half-full for its 9:00 a.m. service. Trixie and I arrived early so I could beat the rush to the front pew. I knew I looked good decked out in true southern style with my powder-blue suit, matching pumps and purse. My wide-brimmed hat had white lace and colorful feathers arranged around the brim. I wasn't sure if people still wore hats, but First Ladies always set the tone. I glanced over at Trixie and smiled proudly. My baby inherited my sense of style. Her dress fit her cute shape nicely, and her jewelry was gorgeous even though she looked as if she went over her budget. As Trixie and I walked up the center aisle, I looked around at the church's modern décor. Pastor Donnelly's wife must have been fashionable. She should rest easy knowing I'll be taking over the reins. Not in a spiritual sense. I was still done with religion, but Trixie needed a father figure. At first, a man of God was not on my radar, but Trixie's situation needed someone who had a deeper insight into the problems that have faced my family for generations.

Trixie and I sat on the front row and placed handker-chiefs over our laps. My mother was a stickler for church etiquette. Because of her, I knew how to maneuver through the toughest boardrooms and church politics. I was ready.

Just before service started, the head usher approached me. She was big, black, and happy. I knew exactly how to deal with her type.

"Excuse me ma'am, this seat is reserved."

"Oh, I'm sorry. I didn't notice a reserved sign," said Tonya.

"No, but the first lady normally sits here."

"Isn't she dead," blurted Trixie.

"Please excuse my daughter. Where would you suggest we sit?"

"How about the third row? It's right behind the elders," said the usher.

"Thank you so much."

"I'm Sis. Washington."

"God bless, we are the Petersons."

Trixie and I made our way to the third row, smiling and shaking hands before we settled into the middle of the row directly across from the podium. I made sure my dress had a little cleavage and that my hat still rested at a cocky angle, "Trixie, make sure your phone is on silent."

"Momma, why did you let that old lady punk you?"

"Trixie, you know better. I'm making allies."

"What do you need allies for?"

"I'm about to get a preacher for a husband."

As service continued around me, I raised my hands at the appropriate time and even dabbed at the corner of my eyes when the singer hit a moving note. Most people would be surprised to learn that my fifteen-year-old had never been to church, but I couldn't get pass my personal experience of listening to the preacher drone on for over an hour about

"One glad morning" when I was her age to at least bring her on special occasions. Even though I was done with religion, sometimes I listened for a few seconds on social media as I scrolled down my page. Pastor Donnelly's church caught my attention the most. He was charismatic and didn't use a bunch of clichés that weren't in the Bible.

When I was in elementary, I wanted to learn more about the man who was also a God and all-powerful. I didn't even blame Him when my parents continued to argue or when my daddy never came home, no matter how much I prayed. I knew it wasn't Him; it was me. After that, I didn't bother God anymore. My mother may have made me go to church, but she could not make me care. I'd sneak out of service and hang with the neighborhood drug dealers who thought paying their tithes would keep them out of jail. Sometimes we would do other stuff, but that was rare. I didn't want to be struck by lightning.

Now, God has more than enough pressure dealing with women waiting on Him to give them a house with a 500-credit score or send them a man when they walk in stores with bonnets and rolls of fat accumulating over their panty lines. True, they probably could get a bed partner, but the few decent men I knew wouldn't go for those types of women. Then again, those women probably didn't know the specifics of a decent man. To them, any man was better than being lonely. #stuckonstupid.

When it was time for the benediction, Trixie had to nudge me back to the present. I'm mad that I missed the part where the first-time visitors stood. I wanted to make sure Pastor Donnelly knew I was present.

"Don't say a word, just smile and appear shy," I said to Trixie as Sister Gloria approached after service.

"Sister Peterson, how did you enjoy service?"

"It's been a long time since I've felt connected to God

like I did this morning. I'm ashamed to admit it, but I needed this today."

"Praise God, are you thinking about joining our family?"

"Choosing a church home is important, but I think I'm being led here."

"Welcome to the family. You and your daughter are a great addition to our church she said, pulling out a comment card to take my information."

"Well, ladies, I see Sister Gloria has talked you into giving Guiding Light a shot. Does that mean I'll be seeing you at Bible study this Tuesday? Our new youth minister is wonderful with the young adults," said Pastor Donnelly, walking up to stand next to Sister Gloria.

"We'll be there," I replied.

"Pastor, why don't we invite the Petersons over to my house for Sunday dinner? Her daughter can hang with my grandbaby."

"That's a great idea, and you can get to know some of our older members," said Pastor Donnelly.

"Thank you, but Trixie and I have a previous engagement."

"Well, I'll see you Tuesday at 7:30," said Pastor Donnelly.

"Yes, Pastor." After service, Trixie and I rode home in silence. We were more than halfway when Trixie brought up the topic of her father again.

"Momma?"

"Yes?"

"I really need you to hook me up with my father?" I reached for the radio, but Trixie caught my hand.

"Please tell me you did not just stop me from turning on the radio in my car?"

"Momma, please, I need him to handle something for me."

"You can't be serious. If he were the kind of man to handle things, don't you think he would be in your life? Why is this light taking so long?" I screamed, frustrated.

"So why isn't he? Can I at least have more than a first name-if you even told me the truth about that."

"Look, Trixie, your father is someone who doesn't care about you or me. It sounds harsh, but that's the facts."

"Well, can I find out for myself?" Trixie asked, turning the radio down.

"Do you."

Trixie grew excited, "Give me the number."

"Find it yourself. You're the one who wants to dredge up the past, acting all ungrateful."

"I bet you don't even know who he is."

"Please don't make me hurt you."

"Go ahead. You're just mad because it's true. I hate you!" Trixie screamed as she hopped out the car.

I hope it rains. I pulled away from the red light as if my teenage daughter didn't just jump out the car. She had money, and she was resilient. I'm the one who needed to keep it together. Dredging up the past was testing my resolve.

***

"We ain't gonna do nothing." This lie, uttered repeatedly while shaving the essential spots, was one of the biggest lies perpetrated by the female race. During the grooming phase, she'd tell herself hygiene always mattered as she executed an extra-wide squat in the shower, then layered oil and lotion, followed by a rummage through her dresser in search of the "good" underwear. If the rendezvous spot was her house, her attire for the evening depended on how long the guy had been around. The longer the connection, the more comfort-able her options-easy to take off. A new guy, had to put in work-tight jeans, bra, the whole nine. The results, however, were the same. A wild night followed by a barrage of unspoken questions. Was I fresh enough? Did he put the condom on soon enough? Will he hear me if I pee? Should I wipe off for another round? Will he spend the night? Should I say anything or get the jump and escort him out? Do I wait for him to call? The dance continued round after round until one day, if she was lucky, he put a ring on it and none of it mattered anymore.

"I don't have any condoms," he muttered, breathing heavily.

"You mean to tell me you can't even afford a pack of Trojans," I said, pushing him off me.

"Wasn't expecting to get this far rich girl," he said kissing me softly on the lips.

"I just don't want to get pregnant," I said, returning his kiss. My first boyfriend and my last love pulled the shirt over his head and stepped out of his shoes.

"Trust me."

EPISODE SEVEN

"ROASTED" CHICKEN

Trixie walked into the youth center and stared.

Outside of the schoolhouse, she rarely interacted with anyone her age, and the center was full of kids. The lobby was a huge open space with see-through classrooms. There were kids playing video games, practicing the piano, and studying in computer rooms. Most of the kids were too busy to pay Trixie attention, but a few girls looked at her curiously. Trixie quickly turned her head. She was not there to make friends with girls who giggled about the latest nail polish from Wet–n-Wild and purchased gloss at the beauty supply store. She wanted to complete her counseling and move on. Wandering towards the back of the center, Trixie noticed a group of teenagers lounging around an outside basketball court. Some guys were taking turns freestyling or slap boxing while several girls stood around on their phones eyeing the boys playing ball.

As she stood at the door watching, a pair of arms reached around Trixie and pushed open the door. He was tall, at least 6 feet with a deep chocolate flavor.

"What's up?"

"Hey," said Trixie.

"Do you have a name?"

"Yea, I'm Trixie. What's up with your tattoo?" asked Trixie noticing the diamond tattooed on his chest with a "V" in the middle.

"It represents my organization, the Millionaires."

"What type of organization is that?" asked Trixie.

"Now, if I told you…"

"I know. You'd have to kill me."

"Nah, I'd have to make you my girlfriend," he said.

"Oh, okay, good one," Trixie said, turning her back.

"Vince, come here, boo. It's your turn." Trixie turned around to see a brown-skinned girl with a lot of curves giving her the evil eye.

"Looks like you already have a friend-boo," said Trixie.

"Don't be like that, she's one of the Millionaires," said Vince pulling out a small notebook and pen. "Give me your number."

"How many numbers do you collect that you have to carry a small notebook," asked Trixie.

"Well, you're my first today," grinned Vince.

"You can put your number in my phone since you don't have one. You ain't slick fronting with a notepad."

"Whatever."

"Vince, outside. You know the rules." Vince nodded his head at Trixie and headed to the basketball court.

"Hello, can I help you?" Trixie turned to see an older man wearing a coach's whistle walking towards her.

"I'm not interested in playing sports," Trixie said.

"No problem, I'm the director of the youth center. Would you like to get signed up for some of our other programs?"

"I'm here to meet with Awana Thompson," Trixie said.

"That's my wife. I believed she's in a meeting right now.

I'm Mr. Lawrence. Let me show you around; she shouldn't be much longer."

"Okay."

Lawrence Thompson was both the owner and director of the youth center. After losing his football scholarship in college, he changed his major to business then worked at a major corporation after graduation. Seven years later, he quit his high-paying job and began working as an assistant coach at a youth center. Now, he and his wife owned six centers in the area.

"What types of activities do you like?"

"I'm not sure."

"Well, this place is a great way to explore. We have sports, music programs, acting, and all types of dance."

"Do you have anything with fashion?"

"Yes. When you finish with Awana, come see me, and I'll get you more information."

Lawrence ended the tour at the back of the building, where most of the offices were.

"This is it, just knock and go in."

Awana's office was classy. The color scheme displayed shades of tan and brown with bursts of orange and mint green. Sculptures and strategically placed plants rounded out the look.

"You must be Trixie. I'm glad you're on time."

"That's all you have to say? I doubt you can help me."

"Do you need help, Trixie?"

"Do you think I need help?" Trixie responded sarcastically as she wandered around the room. Awana's office was different from Mr. Clayton's. His office was sterile and full of items that made him seem pious and narcissistic at the same time. Awana's office had very few personal effects but was warm and inviting.

"I think you need someone to talk to."

"So, you don't mind if I call you by your first name?" Trixie asked, taking a seat.

"Awana or Mrs. Thompson, it doesn't matter as long as you feel comfortable."

"Okay, Mrs. Awana, what's next?" Trixie asked.

"Well, did you read over your confidentiality agreement?"

"I know all about that, everything is a secret."

"Well, not everything. If I think you will harm yourself, other people, or if someone is harming you, I'm obligated to disclose this information," Awana said, pointing to a line in the agreement.

"So, what if I tell you something terrible but not against the law, will you tell my mom?"

"I would encourage you to see the importance of telling your mother, and I would be there to support you. But if you chose not to tell, then that would be your decision."

"I guess that's okay," said Trixie.

"So, Trixie, what brings you to counseling?" Awana asked.

"I had no choice."

"No choice?"

"My mother would beat the crap outta me," Trixie said, taking a mint out of the candy jar perched on Awana's desk.

"Okay, is that what you want to talk about this session?"

"Aren't you going to ask me if my mother abuses me?"

"Does she?"

"I guess not."

"Tell me about Trixie."

"My favorite color is green. I'm intelligent, and I can't wait until I am 18 and I can move out on my own."

Trixie crossed her legs and pulled down her blouse to expose the tops of her breast.

"So, what do you like to do in your spare time?" asked Awana.

"Read and listen to music."

"Hang out with friends?"

"Don't have any."

"Watch TV?"

"Not really."

"Shop?"

"You know it," Trixie said, snapping her fingers. Awana pulled out her notebook and made a few notations.

"Appearance is important. You can't command a presence in scrubs," Trixie said, taking another mint.

"I see."

"Let's take you, for instance. You have an okay shape for your age, but you're not working your hot spots."

"Ok," Awana said, grinning slightly.

"You have a small chest, no offense, so you need a push-up with padding. If you put a few highlights and layers in your hair, it would be banging. You dress okay. You just need your clothes a little tighter, not hoochie tight, just diva tight," said Trixie feeling confident.

"Thanks for the advice. I heard you say the right appearance will help you command a presence. Is attention important to you?"

"Of course, I'm a teenager." Awana didn't comment. She just sat there waiting for Trixie to continue.

"Well, it makes me feel good, powerful."

"Uh, huh," Awana said.

"I like when guys stare at me, it lets me know I'm in control.

"Why do you feel the need to be in control?"

"Control what you can and to hell with what you can't."

"How do you gain control?"

"Why do you people always want to get in my business? It's only the first session.

Awana felt a heaviness in her chest. The years working with rebellious teens as clients were wearing on her. The past few months, she had been thinking about going into practice with a former schoolmate. For most of her cases, she would give expert testimony for various defense attorneys. Although her life would be more hectic, she would be less tempted to develop a personal relationship with the area's troubled kids.

"We can slow down. I do a lot of work with transient youth, so I try to get as much from them as quickly as possible. Are you ok with telling me what brought you here today?"

"I like boys."

"So, do I," Awana said nonchalantly.

"And occasionally, girls."

"I see."

"Sike, did I shock you?" Trixie laughed.

"No."

"If you knew all about me, you'd run the other way."

"Try me," Awana said, leaning forward slightly.

"No, let's talk about what you are hiding from Mrs. Awana."

"No Trixie let's talk some more about you. Underneath the clothes and after the attention, what's left?" asked Awana. Trixie jumped up and thumped her fist on the desk.

"Sit down now, and if you ever get in my face again, you will have some problems," Awana said coolly.

You're not my momma."

"Exactly."

"I'm ready to go," Trixie said with her arms folded.

"That's okay, our time has expired. I'll see you next week."

"Why can't I come back tomorrow?" Trixie asked.

Awana smiled softly, "I see my pro bono clients once a week."

"That's just an excuse, you don't need the money, you drive an SUV like my mother's. I know how much it costs," Trixie said.

"It's not about the money; it's about accountability. Listen, you help me out around here for a couple of hours after school, and I'll give you one additional session a week."

"Okay, but I'm not good with little kids, and I don't do the maid thing."

"Let me share a secret with you. "I'm not too good with little kids either, and you'll help me out wherever I need you. I'll see you-"

"Tomorrow, I'll be here around four," Trixie said.

***

I leaned back and slumped my shoulders. My foot massage felt like heaven.

"Please Momma."

I finally took a moment to relax at the salon after a few hectic weeks, and Trixie was bothering me again about seeing a counselor at the youth center.

"No."

"But why?" Trixie whined. I sat up in the chair and gathered my things. Next time I'm rolling solo.

"I'm sorry, Jen. Give me a minute. Trixie, the answer is no. You can continue with the school counselor or no counselor at all. I'll be at school tomorrow afternoon to pick you up. I'm coming early so I can speak with all your teachers. Your grades had best be up to par," I said.

"You wanted me to go to counseling, and now you're stopping me from going, I just don't get you," Trixie said.

"I'm the parent, so you don't have to 'get me.' Why don't you speak to your counselor about that?"

"You make me sick." I jumped from the massage chair and pulled Trixie from under the dryer. My hands were snug around her neck.

"I can't breathe."

My stylist picked up the rollers that fell onto the floor, "Girl, if you gon' kill her, do it in the hallway," Jen said.

I pulled Trixie into the hallway of the suite, "Do you believe that was appropriate?"

"No, ma'am." I walk back into the salon, glad I paid for a private session. "Jen, here's a hundred dollars to cover your wasted time slot and the rollers. Trixie can do her hair at home since she doesn't appreciate what I do for her."

The next afternoon I walked into Trixie's English class dressed in a wrap-around blouse, skinny jeans, and heels. Anytime I visited Trixie's school, I made sure I was dressed to impress. I didn't have the luxury to wear yoga pants and a spandex shirt like the Caucasian mothers wore. If I tried, I'd be seen as a welfare recipient instead of a pampered house-wife. I already knew Trixie had at least a B in her classes and she hadn't been tardy or absent, so my visit was really a state-ment to her teachers that I was watching.

"Mrs. Peterson, I'm glad you came to speak with me today. I am concerned about Trixie," Ms. Brewster, Trixie's English teacher said.

"Are her grades slipping?"

"No, she has the highest average in the class," Ms. Brew-ster said, looking at her computer.

"Then what's the concern?"

"Well, she has a reputation," Ms. Brewster said.

"You just said that her average is good, so this reputation you believe my daughter has is not affecting her grades. Is behavior a problem?" I said, flipping through Trixie's class folder.

"No, but-"

"Does she cause you any trouble at all?" I asked with barely a glance in Mrs. Brewster's direction.

"No," said Ms. Brewster, flustered. I slammed Trixie's folder onto Mrs. Brewster's desk.

"Then your concern is unmerited. Whatever social issues my daughter may or may not be dealing with is not your concern unless it affects the classroom environment. If that happens, then you let me know. Are we understood?"

"Perfectly, but you know, Mrs. Peterson, maybe you should try adjusting your parenting style. Trixie needs a mother, not an agent. Have a wonderful day."

Ms. Brewster moved to speak with a coworker outside the room. The angel on my right shoulder said be thankful Trixie had a teacher who cared, but since I ran this, I brushed pass Ms. Brewster, clipping her with my shoulder. How dare she question my parenting style? I can't think of anything I've done to cause Trixie to act out at school. I had a reason for what I did growing up. It may not have been the best way, but it kept me looking good and occasionally put food on the table that my momma made sure to eat. Trixie didn't have those problems, nor does she have the toughness it forced me to acquire.

"I do the best I can. I'm definitely a better parent than my mother was," I said aloud as I walked around the building.

"Don't touch me!" I looked up and saw Trixie with her hands spread defensively.

"What the hell is going on here?" I asked, lodging myself in front of Trixie.

"Mama, this is Mr. Clayton, the school counselor."

"Mrs. Peterson, I'm so happy to meet you. I was trying to

get Trixie to understand the importance of attending her sessions," Mr. Clayton said

"First of all, you see me if you are having a problem with Trixie. Secondly, don't ever touch my daughter again."

"Mrs. Peterson, I've tried to be understanding and not report that Trixie hasn't been attending her sessions, but if she doesn't see me tomorrow, I won't have any choice."

"I already have a counselor, you perverted shit," Trixie said. Mr. Clayton turned as red as a sausage link and took a step towards Trixie.

"Please don't make me do it," I said, placing my hand in my purse. I hoped he didn't call my bluff since I hadn't carried a blade since college. Mr. Clayton stood for a moment, then stormed down the hall.

"Sorry about cursing," said Trixie.

"Forget it. Just tell me what happened."

Later that evening, I sat on my bed, staring at the police report I filed against Mr. Clayton. After the confrontation in the hallway at school, Trixie shared with me what happened during her counseling session. The signs of abuse were present-withdrawal, mood swings, but I ignored them. What good was providing Trixie the best of everything if she was too screwed up to enjoy them? For the first time, I acknowledged I did not know what the hell I was doing as a mother. I needed help fast.

EPISODE EIGHT

FALLING

Tonya stretched out on the sofa and propped her head on the armrest, "Trixie turn that music down. Did you try on your clothes for Bible study tomorrow?"

"Yes!" Trixie replied, tempted to turn up the volume to her radio a little more.

"Stop yelling, it's so common."

"I guess it wasn't common when you were yelling at me a minute ago," Trixie mumbled as she walked into the kitchen and took a big gulp of apple juice from the bottle.

"Ma, why we can't ever have no Kool-Aid?"

"Because that's for ghetto folk, which is how you will end up if you keep speaking like that," Tonya said, flipping through the channels on her brand-new flat screen.

"I'm young, and I'm black, and I ain't no bougie sista," said Trixie.

"It's about being intelligent. Anyway, Kool-Aid is too fattening. Not more than a drop of mayo on your sandwich, I saw your thighs jiggling when you walked past me in those hot tail panties. No child of mine needs red underwear," Tonya yelled from the living room.

Trixie took out two slices of wheat bread and low sodium ham then slathered on mayo and two slices of cheese.

"Yes ma'am," said Trixie as she added another dollop of mayo.

Ring... Ring.

"I got it," said Trixie as she jumped over Tonya's legs.

"Hello." Trixie held the phone as the caller breathed into the receiver.

"That Jackee knows how to work it, you go, girl," said Tonya to the television screen.

"Hello, Peterson residence. Hello?"

"Get that money, girl," Tonya screamed.

"Ma, I can't hear, keep it down."

Tonya waved the remote in Trixie's direction, "This is my house, that's my phone, and I'm watching *227*. You keep it down or go to your room. Who is it anyway?"

"Pastor Donnelly."

"What!"

"I'm playing," said Trixie as she slammed down the phone. "Just a heavy breather."

"Probably one of your little friends, I don't want boys calling here. You need to concentrate on your books," Tonya said channel surfing.

"But ma-"

"No, boys. You've had enough contact with boys to last a lifetime."

Trixie stormed off to her room and slammed the door, "That's why I have a man, anyway."

Ring...Ring.

"Hello," Trixie answered quickly in case it was Bryan.

"Ah, ahhh." The caller breathed deeply into the phone.

"If you don't say something, I'm going to hang up," Trixie said, wishing she had caller ID on the phone in her room.

"Trixie," said a breathy voice.

"Yes?"

"I need you," said the breather.

"Who is this?" Trixie asked.

"I need you, Trixie. Oh, yea baby, don't go; talk to me, I'm about to-"

"Whose number is 555–2116," yelled Tonya from the living room. Trixie hung up the phone, blocked her number, then dialed *69.

"Hello," answered a breathy voice.

"Mr. Clayton?"

"Yes." Trixie slumped on her bed, holding the receiver in her hands. Her cell phone rang.

"Hello!" Trixie yelled.

"Girl, what's wrong with you?" Bryan asked.

"Sorry."

"Has somebody been messing with my baby? You know I can't have that," said Bryan.

"Nah, I think it was a wrong number."

"I want to see you tonight," Bryan said, deepening his voice.

"Tonight? I don't think I can." Bryan walked through his apartment, plugging in candle warmers, and tidying the living room.

"Please, it's been a minute."

"Okay, but I can't stay too long."

"I'll be there in an hour," Bryan said. Trixie scrambled out of bed and rummaged through her drawers. She hoped her mother wouldn't notice she was gone. It seemed like ever since Tonya was trying to hook a preacher she went to bed earlier and rarely cavorted around town.

When Bryan drove up, Trixie was sitting on the steps.

"Hey baby," Bryan said. "Why are you sitting outside?"

"Looking at the stars and enjoying the night air."

"Give me a hug, I missed you." Trixie burrowed her head in Bryan's neck.

"I missed you too," Trixie said.

"Let's take a ride," said Bryan, pulling away from the curb. "You don't have a curfew, do you, college girl?"

"No, I'm straight."

During the fifteen-minute drive, Bryan and Trixie rode with the top to his convertible lowered. They listened as the radio station blasted love songs into the night air. Caught up in another of her fantasies, Trixie did not notice as Bryan pulled in front of an apartment building.

"Who lives here?"

"I do. I thought I'd show you my place if that's okay?'

"I guess," Trixie said, hesitating for a moment.

Bryan lived on the first floor of a modest complex. The inside of his apartment was sparse yet tastefully decorated. The crowning glory of the living room was a wall-to-wall sound system stacked high with his favorite music collection. Trixie wandered over to Bryan's CD rack as she tried to relax.

"This is impressive," Trixie said, running her fingers over the CD cases.

"Thanks, my parents were music lovers," Bryan said, fixing drinks in the kitchen.

"You like gospel?"

"Yep, most music evolved from gospel. Besides, it's important to have a strong relationship with God. Gospel music motivates and strengthens me. Are you a regular church-goer?"

"My mother and I just started going. I wish we hadn't," Trixie said, settling on the sofa.

Bryan joined Trixie on the sofa, "Why do you say that?"

"She just started going to church last Sunday, but she's acting all holy when all she wants is a good man."

Bryan picked up the remote and tuned into the jazz station.

"I like the church, and the pastor is kind of cool. Maybe he can change my momma." Bryan lit a scented candle and placed it on the coffee table.

"Wait, your mother is trying to hook up with the preacher?" Bryan said.

"That's not funny."

"So," Bryan said. "You're turning into a church girl, huh?"

"I guess."

"Good, because I'm a church boy. I need a Christian girlfriend."

"Oh, so now I'm your girlfriend," Trixie said.

"If you want to be."

"Hm, I've never had a real boyfriend before," Trixie said, fiddling with Bryan's collar.

"Ha ha, how cute," Bryan said inches away from Trixie's lips. Trixie leaned in to close the distance.

"We need to slow down," Bryan said between nibbles on Trixie's neck. He sat up and pulled his shirt over his head. Trixie ogled his biceps and the indentations of his chest.

"Taking off your shirt is your idea of slowing down?" asked Trixie.

Bryan grabbed Trixie and gave her a tight hug, "It was getting a little warm in here."

"Wanna watch some TV?" asked Trixie.

"Nah, let's just sit back and enjoy the music."

Trixie held herself stiffly against Bryan's chest. It felt weird to be close to him. She'd been close to guys before, but this time she didn't feel in control. It was not an enjoyable feeling.

EPISODE NINE

I DON'T WANT TO BE FREE

alerie pulled into my driveway, but before she could put the car in park, I rushed out the front door.

"I know this is not my best friend. One minute, let me get my glasses," I said, checking out the custom paint on her new Porsche.

"You don't wear glasses. Stop playing around and get in," she said, pulling down the visor and checking her gloss. I hopped into the passenger's side and checked my makeup. I couldn't have my girl trying to step her game up without me.

"You know I always drive, but today is a national holiday. My friend is driving a proper car."

"You called me your friend twice."

"I did not."

"Let me roll back the tape. You said, 'I know this is not my best friend.' And then you said, 'My friend is driving a real car.'"

"If we are going shopping, let's go, please," I said, laughing at Valerie and her touchy-feely ways.

We drove for a few minutes in silence. "What's been up with you lately? How's Trixie?"

"I caught the school counselor she was seeing all up in her face at parent night, and she forged my signature and started seeing a counselor at the community center."

"Wait, did he touch her?"

"She didn't say he did."

"Did you ask her? That is so irresponsible of you."

"You're right. I guess it scared me to hear what she would say. I'll talk with her tonight."

Valerie turned into the parking lot of an upscale business center secluded from the main highway.

"Are we doing an exclusive shopping experience? I hope there is a spa. I need a massage," I said as Valerie killed the engine and turned to face me.

"I know we've talked about this before, but I brought you here so you could speak to someone."

"We've gone over this."

"I get it. You believe you can do this on your own, but you need personal counseling. You almost ruined my husband. Did you ever think exposing him would embarrass me?"

"You knew I would make him pay for what he did to you."

"You went too far, and now I have to help clean up the backlash. You made it seem like he was hiring escorts; he may lose his job.

"He got what he deserved. I may have men who like to do things for me, but they aren't married. You don't have to clean up anything because your divorce attorney will do the cleaning. To hell with half, you're going to take it all."

"What if I don't want to divorce my husband?"

I stepped out of the car, "Well, it's a great thing you're going with me to counseling."

***

I appreciated Valerie's little intervention earlier today, but she didn't understand my world. In the past few weeks, outsiders have questioned my parental guidance multiple times. I've made mistakes, and I will make many more before Trixie and I get better, but that's our business. As far as the world is concerned, we're fine, so they can keep their opinions and half-baked attempts at healing me to themselves. I don't fold. Taking one for the team was a foreign concept to me most of my life. Today would be no different.

I exited the car and checked my makeup in the side mirror. I stood in front of the youth center, then squared my shoulders and walked inside. Either the kids were at school or business was slow because the place was empty. I wandered around until I found Awana's office, then I walked in and slammed the door. Before she could respond, I strode to her desk, pinning her in on one side.

"I take it you're not one of our parents."

"My child doesn't need free services."

"Our services are for anyone who needs help. In the mornings, we have group activities. You look like a yoga or Pilates girl. I prefer step aerobics." I could tell Awana was nervous as she rambled and fiddled with the pen on her desk. I backed off a bit before she called the police. I refused to allow her to stare at me from a position of power, so I took a seat in the chair to the right of her desk instead of sitting across from her.

"I should have you fired for counseling my daughter without my consent."

"Ma'am, I have parental consent from all of my parents. What is your daughter's name? I'm sure this is an error."

"There has been no error. I know for a fact she stopped

seeing the counselor at her school, and this is the only place she mentioned."

"You're Trixie's mother. Tonya, right?"

"Don't clean up your mess. I should have your license revoked."

Awana walked over to her file cabinet and pulled out a manila folder. I eyed her slacks and polo shirt. They were cute but basic with no imagination. She dressed like a woman who played by the rules which meant Trixie was playing games again.

"Tonya-"

"Mrs. Peterson."

"I'm sorry. Trixie never mentioned you were married."

"She shouldn't have mentioned anything to you without my permission."

"I think there has been a misunderstanding. I have a letter signed by you giving me consent to treat your daughter."

I peered at the Consent to Treat form, "This is not my signature."

"What do you mean this is not your signature?"

"Obviously, Trixie forged my name. Isn't it customary to meet with the parent before beginning to treat a minor?"

"I'm sorry. Trixie told me you were not very involved in her life, so you probably wouldn't agree to her sessions."

"When Trixie asked me if she could start seeing a counselor at a youth center, I told her she needed to see a professional with stellar credentials."

Awana walked over to the bookshelf in her office and started slamming stuff on the desk in front of me. "I'm not sure where you went to school-"

"Rice University," I said.

"Good for you, so did my husband. I completed my

undergraduate degree at Texas Southern and my graduate degrees at Purdue and John Hopkins."

"Why wasn't I consulted before Trixie started attending counseling?"

"I'm sure I don't have to tell you how smart your daughter is. When Trixie informed me you were supportive of her receiving services, I should have been more aggressive when reaching out to you. It's just that she was in terrible shape. I don't have kids of my own-"

"Of course, you don't. Look, it's obvious you're qualified. I'll allow Trixie to continue, but I need specific updates on her progress."

"I can give you updates on Trixie's progress within reason. Please understand, she is my priority, and unless she is in danger, I'm not legally obligated to share what happens in our sessions."

"Either you tell me everything I need to know about Trixie's progress or I'm going to the owner. I really hate to have you fired when it's such a simple request, but you're not leaving me another option."

Awana handed me a card from inside her desk, "The address to email your concern is at the bottom of the card. I'm sure my husband will respond to your complaint as quickly as possible. We try to be responsible business owners."

I stood and walked towards the door, leaving the business card. Awana was not a match for me, but I liked that she stood her ground.

"I'll expect your calls every Wednesday at 4 pm. Thank you."

***

Awana sat at her desk staring at the degrees on her shelf.

She'd made a rookie mistake. Tonya was no fool. A complaint from someone like her and her license would be in jeopardy. Trixie had painted a picture of a mother who was self-absorbed with little to no priorities. Tonya, despite her expensive clothing and careful grooming, did not appear to be shallow and selfish, just lost. Awana thought about recommending a different counselor for Trixie, but she seemed contrite after their phone conversation. Trixie knew she was wrong to forge her mother's signature and Awana knew she couldn't let Trixie go-not yet.

Trixie settled in the chair across from Awana and grabbed a mint from the newly filled bowel. "Trixie, what would you like to talk about for this session?" Awana asked.

"My momma is a trip. I don't even know why she had me."

"So, you feel unwanted?"

"Sometimes," Trixie said. Awana pointed to a recorder sitting on the corner of her desk. She started recording after Trixie nodded her consent.

"What is love to you?"

"Caring what that person does in life," Trixie said.

"You don't feel your mother cares?"

"Only when it suits her. When I got in trouble at school, she acted all concerned about my good name, but before that she never took an active interest outside of my grades."

"Sounds like she is concerned about your life."

Trixie stood up and paced around the office, "She only wants to brag on me to her friends," Trixie said.

"Uh, huh."

"I can't explain it, but my mom doesn't seem like a mother."

"Are you a good daughter?" Awana asked.

"What do you mean?"

"You speak a lot about the responsibilities of a mother but what about those of a daughter?

"I guess I haven't been all that great either."

"Okay," Awana said.

"I mean there are some things I do that are not nice, but she never listens to me. All she does is correct my errors." Awana scribbled notes on a legal pad.

"Do you overcompensate because you feel your mother is not paying you a lot of attention?"

"Huh?"

"You find attention elsewhere. Is it with boys?"

"I don't want to talk about it."

"Okay. Well, tell me about the trouble you got into at school," Awana asked.

"I almost had a fight. This girl was saying things about me that were untrue."

"What types of things?" asked Awana flipping through her legal pad.

"It doesn't matter, they were lies," said Trixie.

"And what did you do?"

"I tried to hit her."

"Physical violence is a powerful reaction to something untrue."

"I wished our fifty minutes were up," Trixie said, gathering her things to leave.

"Talking makes the time fly."

"Well, I'm through talking," said Trixie as she walked to the door.

"If this is going to work, you have to open up and be honest with me. I won't like you any less," said Awana.

"There are just some things I'm not ready to discuss. I don't know if I will ever be able to talk about those things."

"Why don't you try writing about them?"

"We'll see," Trixie said, opening the office door.

"I'm only asking you to try. Great job today," Awana said, rubbing Trixie on the back.

After her session, Trixie rushed to her room and grabbed her journal from the nightstand. She dialed Bryan's number, but there was no answer. Bored, she locked her bedroom door and turned on her laptop.

"First, grab the banana at the base." Trixie grabbed the banana. "If you're right-handed, hold the bottom of the banana with your left hand while slowly gliding your hand up the stem. You want this to be sexy, so make sure he knows you are enjoying it by your moans. Not fake porn moans, but you're the greatest in the world. I'm excited to be with you, type moans. You do that for a while, and then you slowly insert-"

RING... RING

"Hello."

"Dang boo, it must not be good if you stopped to answer the phone, said Vince."

"What are you talking about?"

"All that moaning in the background." Trixie swiped the top of her computer screen, closing the video.

"Sorry," mumbled Trixie.

"You were watching porn?"

"I don't know what you mean."

"Stop fronting."

"I ain't fronting. I don't know you like that for you to be all up in my business. Trixie grabbed her journal off the nightstand.

"You want me to call you back."

"You good. I'm just embarrassed."

"Man, everybody watches that stuff."

"It wasn't porn. It was a tutorial."

"You don't have to watch a video. I can teach you whatever you like." Trixie walked over to her dresser and pulled out a black lace bra and panty set.

"Do men like a woman in black or red?" asked Trixie as she reached under her mattress and pulled out a skimpy red nightie.

"A man's favorite color is skin. All that lingerie stuff be for y'all girls."

"I don't know if I'm ready for that."

"Then you aren't ready for nothing. Why are you doing all this?"

"I really like him. I don't want him to think I'm a kid."

"How old is this nigga?"

"Twenty-three. He thinks I'm eighteen."

"Bruh, you wrong for that. You don't even look eighteen."

"Yes, I do."

"No, you don't."

"If you really love him, you wouldn't let him get locked up. You already told me your momma is crazy."

"I didn't lie about my age. I really like him. I won't do anything with him. We are just friends."

"You can chill with me then."

"Boy, please. You have too many girls in your face."

"You think dude is being faithful? A twenty-three-year-old and a fifteen-year-old. If he isn't with you, he definitely with somebody."

"No, he isn't. He's into church and stuff. The other night we were kissing, and he stopped himself. I didn't even ask him to."

"You coming to chill over here?"

"Is it going to be you and the crew because I don't like those girls."

"You know you want me to yourself."

"Boy, shut up." lTrixie hung up the phone and tried on her new bra and panty set. She twirled in front of the mirror, imagining she was modeling for Bryan.

A few days later, Trixie walked into the youth center and rushed into Awana's office. She hoped Awana had time to read her journal. Some of her entries were very personal. Trixie took a seat on the sofa and crossed her legs. Awana took Trixie's journal out of her file cabinet and sat in the chair across from Trixie.

"I'm proud of you Trixie. The letter you wrote was good. Writing is very therapeutic, and it can help you process feelings you may not understand," said Awana as she and Trixie walked towards the lobby of the youth center.

"Yea, it was kind of cool," Trixie said. "Where's all the noise coming from?"

"It's probably a dunk contest. You should go watch it. Some of the boys are talented. The court faces the street, so you can see your mom when she arrives. We'll continue going over your journal at our next session."

"Ok," said Trixie.

Trixie settled on a bench outside the youth center and pulled out the latest street novel to read. Tonya didn't like her reading trashy books because she said they put thoughts in her head, but Trixie grew tired of reading books with "literary" value, so she'd order online and hide the packages in her room. Minutes later, engrossed in a scene where a major drug dealer is confronted by his sidepiece, Trixie didn't notice a flashy sports car cruise by, then make an abrupt U-turn. When Trixie glanced up from her book, Mr. Clayton was in front of her.

"Mr. Clayton, what are you doing here?"

"You haven't been to any of our sessions," he said. Trixie glanced around to make sure that help was in shouting distance.

"Are you psycho? I have a real counselor now, not a pervert."

"But I'm the only one who can help you. You need my special attention," said Mr. Clayton, wiping the sweat running down his face.

"Get away from me before I scream," said Trixie, rising from the bench.

"Don't you walk away from me, we need to work things out," said Mr. Clayton grabbing Trixie's shirt.

"Somebody help me!"

"Hey," screamed Vince, racing towards Trixie with a baseball bat. Startled by the sudden flurry of activity, Mr. Clayton ran towards his car just as Tonya pulled up to the curb.

"What is going on here?" screamed Tonya getting out of the car.

"Mr. Clayton tried to get me to go with him," Trixie said between hiccups.

"Why is he not in jail?" Tonya hugged Trixie and started walking towards the car. Lawrence rushed to their side, "Ma'am, wait a minute. I need to get a statement."

Tonya turned to berate Lawrence for not having adequate supervision at the youth center, but her mind went blank.

Lawrence took a step closer to Tonya. He reached towards Trixie. "Tonya? It's me, Lawrence."

"Get in the car," Tonya snapped as she shoved Trixie towards the car.

"But mom, that's Mr. Lawrence, the youth director."

"Get in the damn car!"

"Tonya, wait. I need her to make a statement," said Lawrence.

"Trixie is not giving a statement. She probably enticed him," said Tonya as she got into the car and drove away.

Lawrence stood, staring at the disappearing car. He could hardly believe he had seen Tonya after all these years and with a teenage daughter.

The next morning Trixie and her mother barely spoke to each other and never made eye contact. Tonya's recent practice of cooking breakfast every morning was the only concession she made towards being a normal family. At the table, Trixie tried to work through her problems like Awana showed her during one of her sessions. She gathered writing paper and a pen from a kitchen drawer.

"Okay, mom, I want us to do an exercise I learned in counseling." Tonya continued to eat.

"I'm going to make a list of the pros and cons of our relationship. Then we need to decide the qualities we want to keep, discard, and those that need repair. I'll start. Well, our first good point is we both take pride in our appearance, and we get to spend time together while shopping. Do you have anything to add?" Tonya stared at her food in silence.

"Oh-kay, well, let's try a point of improvement. I think we need to work on communicating with each other. Since you started hitting on-I mean hanging with the pastor, things have gotten better, but we still need work," said Trixie.

"Mom, can you at least look at me and pretend you care? Don't you love me?" After Tonya didn't answer, Trixie threw the tablet across the table and rushed from the room, "Here, maybe you can use the pad to write out the cons of having a daughter you hate!"

Tonya stared at the notepad in deep thought. She swiped at her tears then entered a single item for each side of the chart.

***

I sat in the driveway of my mother's home biting my

nails. I paid good money for a full set, including my weekly touch-ups, so I knew I was stressed. I needed to speak with my father, but I didn't know where he was living. It had been so long since I'd spoken to my parents, but the pain in my heart was still heavy. I tried to make myself go inside, but I couldn't. Instead, I backed slowly out the driveway.

"I knew you were fast from the beginning walking around selling your body for clothes and to get your hair done," said Theresa Peterson.

"But ma, Lawrence was my first. We love each other," said Tonya on her knees in front of the living room sofa. Theresa walked around the room, anointing the walls and doors. She grabbed a cup from the coffee table and started sprinkling water around the room, making sure most of it landed on Tonya.

"Then where is he now and why you ain't got no ring on your finger?"

"I told you he just needed some time to think, he'll be here and then we'll work it out," said Tonya.

"You are so stupid. You think because you got that fancy education, and all that money saved that boy gon' marry you? He done got what he wanted and now you stuck with a baby."

"Well then, I'll just get a job and take care of my baby alone," said Tonya.

"You just got all the answers, don't you? A man don't want no working woman trying to be the head. They want a God-fearing woman who knows how to take care of a house and cook. I tried raising you right. I just don't know what's wrong with you," said Theresa anointing Trixie.

"The same thing that's wrong you, always mouthing off. If you would have saved some of that energy for the bedroom, maybe my daddy wouldn't have left."

"You take that nasty talk of yours and finish praying for forgiveness in your room. I'll be glad when your dad comes to take you away from here," said Theresa as she picked her bible off the coffee table. "The Lord is my shepherd; I shall-"

EPISODE TEN

BANDWAGON

Y ears ago, it was unheard of. Then it became a closely guarded secret. Now, it's a natural part of life, and only the deliberately stupid or the insanely religious parent believes their teenager is not having sex. Yes, there are the rare kids whose sexual encounters equate clandestine moments either with themselves or with the incognito feature on their cell phones, but to say that your child covers her eyes at the new PG-13 content even when no one is around, is foolery.

Parents of the new breed (gender non-conforming, polyamorous, do what I want brats) have ushered in a wave of get your condoms from me, or I'll buy the room for prom, partially because they realize social media and the current sexual revolution control the narrative. However, not all was lost. A large dose of hope topped with mounds of straight talk may go a long way to curtail natural tendencies. But then again, a belt, a bible, and some anointed oil probably work better.

Trixie stared at herself in the mirror and adjusted her breasts to sit high in her lace bra. She considered wearing something special for her first time, but she didn't want to look easy. She walked out of the bathroom and into Bryan's bedroom. She made herself comfortable on the top of his blanket, legs slightly spread like the pictures online. She took a second to sniff her important parts then leaned back on her elbows.

"Bryan, can you come here? I need help."

"Where are you? I thought you were in the bathroom." Bryan walked into his bedroom and clicked the light switch.

"Can you turn the light back off? Maybe just the lamp."

"Damn."

"I think I at least deserve a hot damn." Bryan ran a hand up Trixie's outer thigh.

"You're definitely hot. What are you doing?"

"What does it look like?"

"It looks like you're trying to get in trouble. I know we haven't talked about this, but are you ready for sex?"

Trixie ran her hand under his shirt, up his chest, "We don't have to go all the way. I like you. You like me. Plus, I need to release a little stress."

Bryan leaned into Trixie, and they fell back onto the bed. Trixie pulled him closer and wrapped her leg around his waist. Bryan flipped on his back and hugged Trixie, "You're so beautiful."

Trixie nibbled on Bryan's ear lobe and kissed his neck, "You like it?"

"You can't tell," said Bryan, running his hands down her back. Trixie kissed her way down his chest, stopping at the waistband of his basketball shorts.

"You don't have to," said Bryan breathing heavily.

Trixie hesitated, "I want to." She rubbed her hand down the front of his shorts, and he arched off the bed, running his fingers through her hair. Trixie kissed along the waistband of his shorts, then applied more pressure to him with her hands.

"Feels good," said Bryan as he lifted and pulled his shorts underneath his butt. He held himself in one hand and gently pushed Trixie's head downward.

"Don't hold me too tight," said Trixie. Bryan ran his fingers through Trixie's hair, using his grip to push her head down again.

"No! Stop! Get off me." Trixie scrambled away from Bryan, elbowing him in the private area.

"Argh!" Bryan yelled, knocking Trixie to the floor.

"Take me home."

Bryan rolled into the fetal position, "Give me a minute," he huffed. "I didn't mean to hurt you. Baby, I'm sorry. I didn't mean to."

"Take me home," said Trixie staring at the floor. Bryan struggled to get off the bed, "You didn't have to hit me in my junk. I hadn't planned to go all the way. I didn't tell you to take off your clothes and get in my bed."

Trixie unzipped her backpack, slipping her legs into her jeans.

"Take me home now, or I'll tell everyone you tried to hook up with a fifteen-year-old girl."

"Who's fifteen? You told me you were eighteen."

"I never told you that."

"But you said you were in college studying psychology. You let me kiss you and I almost-"

"Look, I'm sorry for misleading you. There, now can we go?" said Trixie walking towards the door.

Bryan slipped on his shorts and t-shirt, "Man, I should have never brought you here. I'm a Christian and I-"

"Yea, yea, everybody's a Christian these days, but you sure weren't studying the Word a few minutes ago," said Trixie walking out the door.

SEASON TWO

MY BLACK IS A WEAPON

My black skin is a weapon. Apparently, it sprays people, mostly my pale-faced sisters and brothers, with a vitriol that slowly eats away at their human decency, forcing black men to live in a world that sees us as subhuman. A world that chips at our inner core, whittling us down to a few broken pieces. If we're fortunate, the remaining shards are collected, nurtured, and planted to grow and face the world again. I was one of the lucky ones. When my professional football career went down the drain and Tonya went missing, I wande red through life until I met Awana. Her love and trust redeemed me. Many men never find that one person; most meet angry black women dealing with their own set of societal perceptions or the upwardly mobile sista looking for the perfect mate when the average black man is not enough.

I never wanted to be that dude, not to her. I tried and failed. Now, I'm about to break the heart of my queen. How easy it would be to pull out the driveway and leave my troubles in Houston while I pretended I hadn't just seen my first love and our teenage daughter. I could ignore the situation then deny parentage if the issue was forced, but the truth is I want my daughter. I'm also afraid of losing the life I struggled to build.

It took years for Awana and me to merge our unique backgrounds and families to create a successful union. Awana came from an upper-middle-class family and was an only child while I grew up with five siblings, two of whom my parents adopted. Growing up, my life was a series of family outings, recitals, and athletic events. Awana's childhood was different with two doctors for parents and a live-in housekeeper. My job was to cherish her and protect her dreams as her husband. Now I had to tell my beautiful wife that the one dream we failed at is another woman's reality.

"Baby, I have something to discuss with you." I sat next to Awana on the living room sofa and placed her cell phone on the end table.

"What is this all about? You made me cancel my last appointment," said Awana.

I slid closer and grasped her hands, "There is no easy way to say this, but I- well, you know how I told you I was a talented athlete in college before my injury."

"Lawrence, I know all that," said Awana.

"Those Texas Southern girls would sweat the players from Rice like crazy. Boy, I remember one semester a group of girls-"

"Please don't remind me. I still see my mother swooning when I told her I enrolled at TSU."

"It definitely wasn't any easier when you told her you were marrying a Rice dropout with a bum leg. Thank you for standing by me and loving me. Those were some tough years."

"You turned it around, and now my parents love you."

"Nah, they love this five thousand square foot house you made me buy."

"You know my daddy thinks of you as his son. Either way, you're always my number one."

God, I love this woman. I leaned over and kissed her on the forehead, "It's an honor being your husband."

Awana chuckled and squeezed my hand. I couldn't gather the energy to return the affection. My insides felt like jelly.

"Aww, I love you, baby. Are you dying because it's not our anniversary or my birthday?"

"When I chased after the man who tried to lure Trixie in the car, I saw my old girlfriend from college. It was Trixie's mother."

Awana stared at me. She knew. I could feel it.

"I have a fifteen-year-old daughter, and I think it's Trixie." I tried to read Awana's eyes, but I couldn't see past my own fears.

"I know it's Trixie."

"What?"

"Yes."

"Wait a minute," said Awana standing. "You never shared you had gotten a girl pregnant, and now you're saying Trixie may be your daughter?"

"Trixie is my daughter. I didn't know where Tonya was. I didn't even know if she kept the baby."

"It doesn't matter. In ten years of marriage, you couldn't tell me you might have a child running around somewhere!"

"I'm sorry. You just don't know what it feels like to be a parent and not know where your child is."

"Maybe you didn't want to know. Maybe you just wanted to be another trifflin negro."

I jumped from the sofa, swiping the magazines off the coffee table, "That's not me, and you know it! Tonya is not some welfare momma trying to cheat the system. She has more than both of us."

"Trust me, she is struggling, and so is Trixie. Do you have any idea how screwed up Trixie is? How not having a father in her life-you know what, I can't have this conversation with you right now."

"Wait a minute what kind of stuff is she going through?"

"You know I can't give you that information."

"I'm her father! For fifteen years, I did not have a say in her life. I deserve to know what is going on with my child.

"All you need to know is that little girl, in a teenage body, needs help, and it will take all of us, especially with a mother like Tonya."

"Don't do that."

"Do what? Speak the truth?"

"Act insecure and say nasty things about Tonya. She is still the mother of my child, and we have to work together."

"You're berating me over the woman who kept your daughter from you? She is half the reason Trixie's screwed up. I'm looking at the other half. That's how you like 'em, huh? High maintenance with a side of trashy hood."

"You need to stop right there. I just got Trixie in my life, and no one will ruin this. No one is more important to me than Trixie. You need to swallow your jealousy and act like my wife."

"Why is it men always revert to calling women jealous when we tell the truth? Jealous for what? You're mine."

"I'm not talking about all that."

Awana shoved me in the chest, "So why am I jealous? Do I have a reason to be?" she asked.

"Because she can have children. I told you after the third miscarriage you did not need to counsel kids. It's like you obsess over them, always complaining about how bad their parents are. You find stuff to point out, so you can convince yourself you could do it better if you were their parent. But you're not a parent, so you need to stop being critical of those who are trying."

"You've been a daddy for five seconds, but you have it all figured out. I work at a youth center in the hood! I ain't making stuff up, so don't make it seem as if I am developing unhealthy relationships with my clients. And don't you dare try to make me seem crazy because I lost my babies."

"I didn't say that."

"It was hard. You don't know how it felt to have your body turn against you. To fall in love instantly only to have it snatched away. I am a mother. I'm a mother, damn it!"

Awana collapsed on the sofa in tears. I moved to embrace her, and she elbowed me in the face.

"Get away from me. I'm fine."

"Baby." Awana stormed out of the living room.

I trailed behind her attempting to apologize. She finally stopped and stared at me as I tried to explain my position. After a few, I realized her body was standing in front of me, but our souls were disconnected.

***

The windowpanes rattled as I pounded on Tonya's front door. I should have contacted my attorney before I came here, but this conversation was past due.

"Tonya! Tonya!"

"I'm calling my attorney and getting a restraining order," said Tonya swinging open the door. I brushed past her and stormed down the hall into the sitting room.

"Sit," I commanded, pointing to the spot farthest from me.

"Don't come to my house trying to boss me around. Funny, you know where to find me now."

I clasped my hands to avoid grabbing her.

"I'm the one asking the questions. Why didn't you tell me you were back in Houston, and why was yesterday my first time seeing our daughter?"

Tonya walked to the sidebar and poured a finger of liquor. She pointed towards the glass.

"You're a drunk now?"

"I usually reserve this for my clients." I watched her stroll over to the sofa, glass in hand. Inwardly I flinched, positive the glass would come flying my way any moment.

"Lawrence, you chose not to be in her life, so I didn't owe you information concerning my location."

"I chose not to marry you when you wanted me to, that had nothing to do with not wanting to raise my child." Tonya sat on the edge of the sofa. *Sip*.

"Same thing."

"For someone who hated her mother's religious beliefs, you sure stuck to them when you got pregnant," I said, pacing the room.

"I was a virgin, and my mother threatened to disown me. What did you expect?" *Sip*.

"I expected you to understand the point of view of a man with a pregnant girlfriend and no job prospects. After I got injured, I lost my football scholarship and had to sit out of school for a semester. Hell, I got back in, but I had to work full time just to take two classes in college.

"Well, I didn't know that."

"Because you left with my child!"

"You left me first." *Sip*.

"Will you put the drink down and act like you care? I always intended to come back for you. I needed time to clear my head. How could I focus on school and raise a family?"

Tonya stared at me as if she wanted me dead, "The same way women do it every day. We could have done it together. I could have held you down until you graduated and got a better job."

"That's not what a man does," I said, dropping my head.

"Maybe not, but that's what a black woman does."

I stood and rested my forehead on the mantel of the fireplace. When I raced over here, I intended to rip Tonya to shreds and warn her of the fight ahead. I expected anger, a knife to the chest, but her silence was killing me, "So, now what?" I asked.

"I don't know."

"Well, Awana and I have talked, and she understands that I want a relationship with my daughter."

"You spoke to Trixie's counselor about this?"

"She's my wife."

"Well, ain't that a-."

"I'd like to spend as much time as I can with Trixie." Tonya walked over to me and put a hand on my back.

"That's not a problem. She needs a male figure in her life."

"I   want   custody."

"You can't be serious."

"You've had her to yourself for fifteen years, and I don't think you've done the best job raising her. It's my turn."

"Get out."

"You can see her whenever you want. We can share the holidays.

Tonya blinked several times. The last time I saw her cry was when I told her I couldn't marry her. My heart fluttered, and I felt a moment of remorse as I walked out of the house. When the front door slammed behind me, I felt as if my past just punched me in the face.

EPISODE ONE

DEADBEAT

I felt like a semi-truck hit me; the kind that transports blocks of ice because my bedroom was as cold as a walk-in freezer last night. A day later and I still felt the chill. When we first got married, like most couples, Awana and I vowed we would never go to bed angry. Over the years, I realized that although we may have verbally resolved our issues before going to sleep, there were moments, even during intimacy, when we withheld some part of ourselves. Last night, Awana made no effort at reconciliation. I knew I was harsh with her yesterday, but I needed my wife-her arms to hold me and her breasts to cushion the pain in my heart. I longed to hear her say I would be a wonderful father, that she would embrace Trixie as her daughter, and together, we would repair the loss of not having me in her life. Instead, she kept to her side of the bed, and I kept quiet, pretending to be strong. When I arrived at the center the next morning, her office was empty. I spent my day taking care of odd errands around the outside of the building so I would not cave and call her. This was the third time I swept the sidewalk. I was in terrible shape.

"Go ahead, call the people on me, I don't care." I looked up to see Trixie standing on the sidewalk a few feet away.

"Trixie, what are you doing here, shouldn't you be in school?"

"Whatever," said Trixie crossing the street.

"Wait, Awana and I were worried about you, come inside."

"Why did my mom freak out when she saw you yesterday?" asked Trixie walking past me inside the community center.

"I think it's best if we wait and discuss that with your mom," I said as Awana rushed towards Trixie.

I guess she wasn't too distraught, I thought staring at Awana. Her pantsuit fit in all the right places; she looked refreshed and sexy.

"I'm glad you're okay. I was worried about you," said Awana, barely looking at me as she followed Trixie into the office.

"I'm cool," said Trixie. She looked relieved at the fact that we weren't making a huge deal over her skipping school.

"Do you know the man who tried to accost you yesterday?" I asked.

"He's my school counselor."

Awana sat in a chair next to Trixie, "What's going on? Was he trying to kidnap you?"

"Nah, he's just freaky, but I can handle him," said Trixie.

"Trixie, this is very important. Has he ever tried anything with you?" said Awana clasping Trixie's hand. Trixie glanced at me and sat silently,

"Lawrence, can you give us a minute?" asked Awana.

I glared at Awana then eased toward the office door, leaving a slight crack.

"Well, for our first session-" I leaned my head against the wall and listened to Trixie recount the events of what took place during her encounters with Mr. Clayton. When she got to the part where he pushed her head in his lap, I crashed through the door.

"Damn it, I could strangle Tonya." Awana stood up, blocking Trixie. "You were listening to our conversation?

You know my sessions are confidential."

I stared at Trixie. *This is my daughter.* I knew I should wait until Tonya spoke with Trixie, but I could not risk her poisoning her against me.

"What's going on here? Why is everyone so upset?" asked Trixie.

"Let's call Tonya so we can discuss things," said Awana moving to pick up the phone.

Trixie stared at me, then at Awana. "This is stupid," she said.

"Lawrence, wait for Tonya," said Awana dialing the number.

"Can somebody please explain what's going on?" asked Trixie pressing the button to hang up the phone.

"I'm your father, Trixie."

Idiot, I thought as I stared at Trixie. What a way to break the news.

"No, you're not."

"Great job, Lawrence. I thought we agreed to let Tonya speak with Trixie," said Awana.

"The timing matches, and I was your mother's first."

"You're lying. My momma was a hoe. She told me so herself."

"Trixie!" said Awana. Trixie cast a pleading look at Awana. "He's your husband. Make him shut up."

I wasn't surprised Trixie thought her mother whored around. Tonya had a sexuality most people envied. She might not be afraid to use sex as a weapon, but she was never a prostitute. In the loosest sense, all of us were in the sex trade. Men expect sex and the occasional domestic act for the money give they gave their love interests. Women understand that because they created the game.

"Trixie, I'm sorry you had to find out this way. I wanted all of us, including Tonya, to sit down and talk through everything."

"You abandoned me fifteen years ago. Talking is the last thing on my mind."

"Trixie, please wait," said Awana grabbing Trixie's hand.

"Did you know?" asked Trixie, jerking away.

"Not until yesterday. If you don't want to talk now, at least let me take you home," said Awana picking up her keys.

"Does my mother know?" I took a deep breath and sat in the chair Trixie abandoned. "I talked to her yesterday. She thinks you should stay with me and Awana for a while."

"Now I know you're lying. My mother would never give me up the way you did. I hate both of you; stay the hell out of my life." Trixie pushed past Awana and left office.

"That didn't go well, but at least she knows," I said.

Awana walked over to me and slapped me across the face, "You just undid weeks of hard work. That was a very troubled girl who ran out of here. How could you do this without speaking to me? And why didn't you tell me you went to that woman's house?" said Awana.

"When I came back last night, you kept your back to me in our bed. Our bed should be neutral ground. I went to Tonya's last night because she is the mother of my child."

"I have a few vivid descriptions for Tonya, and none of them begin with mother."

"You don't have the right to judge my mother. You're not perfect," Trixie said, reentering the office.

I jumped to my feet, "Baby!"

"Don't call me that; you don't even know me. I want a blood test done."

"No problem," I said, grinning.

"Ain't nothing funny. I'm just getting my life straight and now this. Adults are just as jacked up as kids." Trixie walked to the office door and paused with her hand on the handle, "I don't appreciate you lying on my mother."

"I'm not lying. Will you just hear me out, please?"

Trixie stood by the door with her arms folded, staring at me. She looked so much like Tonya I felt like crying as old emotions resurfaced. I moved to the other side of the room to give Trixie her space, took a deep breath, and prayed my words came outright.

"Your mom and I grew up in Sunnyside together. She was the bomb back in the day," I chuckled, remembering how far out of my league she was when we were younger.

"Uh, okay," said Awana. I grinned and winked.

"We were all dirt poor, but your mother was different."

"She never told me anything about you or her life," said Trixie.

"She was proud and hated being poor. Her dad almost went bankrupt trying to please her with the best of clothes and a private school education. Then her parents split."

"What happened after they divorced?" asked Awana.

"Tonya started letting older guys buy her stuff and pay her a lot of attention. Some stuff she kept and others she sold. She and I never hung out, but I saw her around and heard a lot of rumors." I observed Trixie. I didn't know how honest I should be with her or how much she already knew.

"You tryna be nice about it, but I already know how she paid for her stuff," Trixie said.

"I don't know how far she went with the other guys, but she hadn't been with anyone sexually until we started dating."

"In college?" asked Trixie.

"Yes, it was her junior year at Rice. I always liked your mother, but she was out of my league."

"I guess you were too broke for her," said Awana.

"Anyway," said Trixie rolling her eyes. Women rarely accept the truth. They would rather use their time wondering if a man liked them instead of taking his actions at face value. If he wants you, he's coming. If he doesn't, then he's not interested or not ready. Either way, women need to stop wasting time. Tonya knew her time was valuable. She didn't care that I was popular at school or a top prospect. I worked hard to get with her. It was a great relationship while it lasted. I hadn't intended for it to end. She was my forever girl.

"I was an NFL hopeful, so I asked your mother to manage my money when I made it big. I was clowning around, but she was serious. She learned a lot from working with different firms in college. She saved her student loan money and made contacts during her internships. We would meet in the library, and she would talk for hours about growing my money. I wasn't paying attention; I just wanted her to let me take her out. Finally, she did."

I paused for a moment, then walked over to Awana and placed my hand on the small of her back.

"One night, at the beginning of our senior year, things got heated, and we made love. When it was over, Tonya freaked because I didn't use a condom. When she told me she was pregnant, I lost it and disappeared. When I finally contacted her, one of her suite mates told me she took her finals early and opted out of the graduation ceremony."

"Wow," said Awana.

"I tried contacting her parents, but they wouldn't give me any information. A neighbor finally told me she went to live with her father's sister.

"You knew where I was. You just said it."

"Trixie, I swear I tried to find you. We didn't have social media back then, and Tonya's parents wouldn't tell me a thing." I stepped closer to Trixie, entreating her with my eyes.

"I didn't know Tonya had returned to Houston to live. I wanted you. Baby, I promise."

"Listen, we've had a tiring two days. Trixie, I know there are more questions you need answered so let me take you home. We can find another time to talk," said Awana.

"No, I'll catch the bus, I need to think."

"I don't want you on the bus; it's dangerous," I said.

"I've been catching the bus by myself since middle school. I don't need someone who can't find his own child playing daddy."

"Stop by tomorrow after school. We can talk then," said Awana ushering Trixie out the door. My heart pounded in my chest. What if she walked out of the door and never returned?

"Maybe we can all have dinner?" I asked.

"I don't think so. Right now, I don't want to be around any of you. You should have never punked out and quit looking for me." After Trixie walked out of Awana's office, I punched the wall next to the door.

"We have to call CPS; Tonya is unfit. What kind of mother would allow her child to be mauled?"

"I'm sure Tonya handled it, but I will follow up with my contacts anyway," said Awana.

"I ought to go to the school and jack him up for putting his hands on Trixie."

"Lawrence calm down, we need to talk to Tonya and let her take the lead on this situation," said Awana.

"Lead what? The only thing she can lead is my child into a back alley to suck-"

"No one said anything about that," said Awana.

"Well, isn't it obvious? It's what Tonya did."

"You know I can't divulge the content of my sessions with Trixie, so don't go there. It will be hard when I have to refer her to another counselor." Awana's office door flew open, hitting the wall next to it.

"You told him my personal business?" Awana stepped closer to Trixie. "I would never. Our sessions are confidential, even if he is my husband!"

Trixie grabbed the jacket she left on the chair, gripping it close to her chest like a shield. I stood rooted in place, too ashamed to speak. "You can't be my counselor anymore?" she said.

"I'm sorry, but our relationship is complicated now that I know you're my stepdaughter."

"You mean I'm too complicated. I hate you," Trixie cried, racing out the office.

***

Trixie stood outside the doors to the church, afraid of the welcome that waited inside.

"Hello."

"Hey," said Trixie.

"Why are you calling me Trixie?" asked Bryan.

"So, you still recognize my voice."

"Look, I don't have time for games."

"Wait, don't hang up, please, I... I."

"Trixie, are you crying, what's wrong?"

"My... my mom... and my... dad," stuttered Trixie.

"I stopped by the church for a few minutes to grab a few things. Can you meet me there?"

Bryan's office was small yet organized. It was obvious from the various church pictures that he loved his job as a youth minister. On his desk was a portrait of him and his dad dressed in their Sunday best along with a picture of Bryan in the pulpit delivering his first sermon. His dedication to Christ was also evident in the many cards and thank you gifts scattered throughout the office.

"Bryan," said Trixie peeking her head through the door.

"Come on in Trixie. You got here quickly."

"I was close when I called. Thank you for seeing me, I needed to talk."

"Hi, Trixie, I'm the interim youth pastor," said Shelia stepping into the room. Trixie eyed Shelia's curvy body in her plain jeans and platform shoes.

"I'll come back," said Trixie.

"This is Shelia; she's assuming my position for a short time. I asked her to sit in on our conversation."

"I don't know her to be all in my business. Can you ask your girlfriend to leave?" said Trixie.

"I'm not his girlfriend. I understand your need to speak with Bryan alone, but it's a rule for our church to have two people present. I'll wait outside while you two talk. I promise I won't eavesdrop," said Shelia as she cracked the office door.

Bryan sat behind his desk and fiddled nervously with his computer screen. "Okay, now tell me why you're upset." Trixie wandered around the office, looking at the pictures and running her fingers over the books on his shelf.

"Does she know about us?" asked Trixie.

"Of course not."

"I met my father for the first time today."

"Man, that's serious. How are you feeling?"

"He's married to my new counselor." Bryan leaned deeper into his office chair and took a long look at Trixie.

"You sure know how to do it big."

Trixie took a seat in one of the office chairs, "Well, you know how I roll," said Trixie attempting to laugh.

"Seriously, I'm sure you're overwhelmed.

How are you dealing with all of this?"

"I feel confused. I always imagined that one day I would open the door and there he'd be, furious he never knew about me. What a joke. He knew about me all along. He just didn't want the burden."

"Listen Trixie, I know it doesn't seem like it now but you and your father can have a relationship one day."

"I know, but I feel so unwanted. I feel like my mom only deals with me because she'd go to jail any other way."

"You're not alone or unwanted, just give it time. Your mom loves you the best way she knows how. She probably didn't have the best example from her parents," said Bryan moving from his chair.

"I miss talking to you. You help me forget about my problems," whispered Trixie. Bryan knew Shelia was in the hallway, so he casually moved Trixie toward the door.

"Trixie, God loves you. He's the only man you need right now."

"So, what if God is a woman?"

"Ha ha, you get the point," said Bryan as he ushered Trixie out of his office.

"Sorry if I was rude earlier," said Trixie.

"It's ok. We all get a little testy sometimes. Just remember, as a believer, you may encounter obstacles that test your faith. Still, God is always there, and I'm an excellent listener if you want to stop by," said Shelia giving Trixie a hug.

"See you in church Sunday and stay off the bus," said Bryan as Trixie walked out of the building.

***

Trixie raced to sit on the sofa when she heard the garage door open. She folded her arms and waited for Tonya to enter. "And where have you been all this time, little lady," said Trixie.

"You so need to chill out, we were just hanging," Tonya said in her best teenage voice.

"Were you with Pastor Donnelly?"

"Yes, but don't get too excited."

"My mommy got a boyfriend, my mommy got a boyfriend," chanted Trixie as she did the cabbage patch.

"I haven't had one of those in years."

"Ma, chill out, I got you. All you have to do the next time he comes in for a kiss is grab him by the head-"

"Girl don't play with me. Sit down. We need to have a talk," said Tonya.

"Ssh, *227* is coming on."

EPISODE TWO

FIRST DATE

Theresa stepped onto the front porch when she saw the car lights flicker through her window.

"Mrs. Peterson, please hear me out. I want to make things right," I said, stepping out the car. I watched as Theresa walked down the driveway away from the house.

"Are you prepared to marry my daughter," she snapped.

"No. I mean, yes, just not right now. I need to find a job and-"

"Pitiful excuses, you're not even a man," said Theresa walking away.

"Just give me a chance. Tonya and I will move in together, and I'm sure we'll have enough money saved before the baby comes." I was so desperate I felt like dropping to my knees and wailing.

"And continue to live in sin? Where? Surely not here, there are no sinners in my house."

"Where's Tonya, I need to speak with her? I need her to know I love her and our baby. I will make things right for us."

"Leave."

I pushed passed Theresa screaming for Tonya, "Please, is she here? Can I speak to her?

"I said, there-are-no-sinners-in my house,"

***

I placed the folder from my attorney under the car seat and rushed into the restaurant. I never thought I would be a statistic, another black man using the courts to mediate my family issues. My first task was to put myself on child support. I know Tonya has the financial piece handled, but now that I have a daughter, I refuse to be a deadbeat. I'm going to pay support until I make up for the past fifteen years. Then I'm going to work on building a relationship with Trixie. I took a seat at the table across from Awana and grabbed a piece of bread out of the basket. I wasn't hungry, but my stomach was knotted.

"Lawrence are you sure you don't want me to leave so you and Trixie can spend some time alone?" asked Awana.

"No, you're as much a part of this as I am. If we're gonna seek custody of Trixie, you need to strengthen your relationship with her."

"I know you don't want to hear this, but I don't think that is necessary. If Tonya attends parenting classes and Trixie keeps up her sessions, things will be much better."

I banged my fist on the table in frustration, "I want my daughter! I have been out of her life too long. I intend to be there 24–7 from this point on."

"Well, I guess that point begins now," said Awana putting a smile on her face as Trixie approached the table.

The first half of dinner was stilted and resembled small talk at a cocktail party. However, midway through, we lapsed into a peaceful pattern, and I was feeling optimistic.

"Can you bring my daughter the cheesecake?" I asked as the waiter removed the main course.

"If you want to call me daughter, whatever, but I'm not ready to call you, dad," said Trixie.

"Lawrence and I understand that this is a time of transition for you. There is no need to rush anything. Maybe you and Lawrence can attend some of your sessions together," said Awana.

"You would counsel your own husband?" asked Trixie.

"As much as I enjoy being your counselor, I have to refer you to a colleague of mine. I think you two will get along well."

"How much of my business will she have to know," asked Trixie.

"Only what you share. But I think you will see the more you share, the more stable your emotions will become."

"And having a suitable home environment is helpful, right baby?" I knew I was pushing her, but I was desperate.

"That is one of the key ingredients," she said.

"Well, my mom and I are getting along better. Since we started attending church, things changed. We spend more time with each another, and she gets on my nerves like a real mother."

"Well, that's great Trixie, I'm so proud of you," said Awana. I pushed my dessert plate away from the edge of the table and placed my hand over Trixie's.

"I'm glad that Tonya is trying to get herself together. If anyone can do it, she can. She has willpower, but I question if it's enough." I ignored Awana, shifting in her seat and clearing her throat to get my attention.

"So much time has passed, and you're practically an adult now. I think you need to be in a stable environment. Trixie moved her hand and scooted her chair back from the table.

"I can't leave my mother. I think it would say that I don't have faith in us. We just need more time.

"But what about-"

"We can take things slowly like Trixie suggested. All of this is new for everyone, and emotions are running high. Let's table the discussion for tonight and let things happen naturally," said Awana.

I quickly paid the bill and met up with Trixie and Awana outside the restaurant. Awana's intervention hurt my feelings, but I knew she was concerned Trixie would balk at the attempts I made at building a father-daughter relationship if I pushed too hard.

"Trixie, would you like to have dinner tomorrow? Nothing fancy, but you can come by the center and grab a bite," I asked.

"Thanks, but my mom cooks for us now."

"What about this weekend, the black expo is in town? Awana loves to spend money on clothes when she goes there."

Trixie stopped walking and turned to face me.

"Stop trying to rush me. I'm not a kid, and I know my own mind. I don't even know if I want to get to know you. I don't like how you've been putting my mom down. I'm not stupid. You've been throwing shade all night. She may not be the perfect mom, but she was there for me, not you."

"I told you why I wasn't there. Your mom-."

"This is not some Hollywood movie. This is my life."

I watched Trixie rush to a small-sized BMW then turned towards Awana, "Are you kidding me. Tonya bought her a BMW. Does she have a license?"

"You okay," she whispered. I brushed past her in silence.

***

Trixie opened her front door and peered into the living room. She thought her mother would be sitting on the sofa waiting to grill her on dinner with Lawrence and Awana, but the house was quiet. The television and lights were off, and the kitchen and backyard patio were empty. She had no idea why she moved soundlessly down the hallway towards her mother's room. She could hear Pastor Donnelly through the speaker of her mother's phone.

"Thank you so much for calling me back," said Tonya.

"It's no problem. If you need to take time off from volunteering, I understand," said Pastor Donnelly.

"I hated my mother so much," Tonya said. "I wanted to hurt her any way I could. When I told her, I was going to have an abortion, she hit the roof. She called me all kinds of names and kicked me out of the house."

Trixie peeped into Tonya's bedroom. She saw Tonya sitting on the side of the bed with a wad of tissue in her hand.

"Have you noticed whenever I try to discuss your father, you ignore me?"

"Because he was right to get away from my mother; we both were. I didn't want any connections to my mother. The child in my stomach was another reminder of my screwed-up family." Tonya walked to her bedroom door and peered down the hall. She thought she heard shuffling, so she walked further into the living room. She saw Trixie sitting on the sofa. "Trixie, I didn't know you were home. How was dinner?"

"Why do you care since you hate me so much?"

"What are you talking about? I don't hate you. Did something happen tonight? That's why I didn't want you to go." Tonya threw her cell phone on the sofa and attempted to hug Trixie.

"I heard you. You didn't want me. Well, I don't want you either." Trixie spun around and marched to her room. Tonya rushed behind her.

"I only meant that I was scared to have a baby because there is a curse on the Peterson women."

Trixie shut her bedroom door and grabbed a duffle bag out of her closet.

"I'm sorry. Please give me a chance to explain. I love you."

Trixie stuffed her bag full of clothes and took the cash off her dresser, "Can you give me some time? Please, mom? I'm gonna take a nap."

"Promise we'll talk later?" asked Tonya through the door. Trixie opened her window and threw her duffle bag to the ground.

"Call Vince," said Trixie as she hopped into her SUV.

"What's up."

"Hey."

"Bout time you called me back. How'd it go with your sugar daddy? I hope you didn't wear his heart out." said Vince.

"I ain't for all of that right now."

"What's wrong? Why don't you come over here?"

"What would your mom have to say about that?"

"She doesn't live here. I stay with my older brother."

"Your brother won't mind?" asked Trixie.

"Nah, long as you chip in on the food, but I got you like that."

"I guess," said Trixie.

"You can crash on the sofa, or I can sleep in my brother's bed. He's hardly here, anyway."

"But you don't even know me," said Trixie surprised.

"Let me worry about that. Besides, you'd be crazy to play me. I'd get my girls to jack you up."

"Please. Just give me your address." Half an hour later, Vince met Trixie in the parking lot outside of his apartment.

At first, she fiddled around, trying to stall before getting out the car. The neighborhood was in a low-income area, and everywhere she drove, tough-looking people stood around. Vince's apartment was not the type she was used to seeing. It had two stories and about six units, all of which had crooked air conditioners in the window.

"I ain't know you was rolling like this," said Vince opening the door for Trixie. Trixie stepped out of the SUV and grabbed her bag. "My mom bought it after my school counselor rolled up on me at the bus stop.

"She couldn't buy a Honda?"

Trixie walked into Vince's apartment and tried not to appear squeamish. The apartment was clean but had a faint Clorox and Pine-Sol smell. It was obvious Vince went out of his way to make Trixie feel at home. Two paper plates and a bag of hot fries sat on a crate next to the TV. Vince grabbed the plates and hot fries and sat next to Trixie on the sofa.

"You want something to drink? I got some coke in the refrigerator."

"I'm ok."

"So why you over here on my side of town with your scary self?"

"What I got to be scared of?"

"Be honest. You didn't want to get out the car."

"I mean, I done been to the hood before."

"I ain't talking about passing through to get to the free-way." Vince poured hot fries onto their plate.

"Do they have shoot outs over here," asked Trixie.

"We do, but if you not caught up in that lifestyle, you should be ok. Anybody can get hit, but why waste time thinking like that." Trixie settled onto the sofa and held her plate out for more fries. She and Vince talked for hours. She didn't share much about her life because she didn't want him to think she was spoiled, but she learned a lot about him.

The first time she met him, she thought he was the typical thug raised by a single mother. When he told her both his parents were a part of his life, her messed up situation was clearer.

"I started selling drugs and running with my crew to get away from all the back and forth my parents were doing."

"Where was your brother?"

"He stayed with some friends until he got this place." Trixie's phone vibrated. It was Tonya. Trixie ignored the text, and after the third call, put her phone on airport mode.

"How long can you stay," asked Vince.

"It's whatever."

"That's what I like to hear. Let's play video games."

Over the next few days, Trixie and Vince played video games and listened to music into the early morning. Although Trixie was afraid to stay over at Vince's apartment, she made sure she spent less time at home. When she did make it home, Tonya was normally asleep. In the morning, she was dressed and out the house before Tonya rose in the mornings.

After several days of dodging Tonya, Trixie reached out and hit the snooze button. 8:35.

"I knew I shouldn't have drunk that Tequila. Now she gon' be up before I get out the house," said Trixie scrambling out the bed.

"Trixie, I cooked breakfast," said Tonya halting Trixie's progression out the door.

"Whatever."

"Trixie, what's going on? Ever since the dinner with Lawrence and Awana you've been acting strange. Did they do something to you?"

"Stop pretending like you care."

"What are you talking about? I explained what I meant on the phone with Pastor Donnelly. Let's sit down and work this out. We can make a list like you learned in counseling. At least eat some breakfast," said Tonya placing a slice of bacon on a plate in front of Trixie.

Trixie picked up the bacon and chomped in Tonya's face, "Satisfied?"

EPISODE THREE

PAYBACK IS A MUTHA

Trixie entered Vince's apartment and settled on a rundown sofa positioned between two chairs. On the wall above was a lopsided water painting his mother brought over the one time she visited him and his brother. There was not much to the apartment. Its prize possession was a PS2 resting on a crate, yet to Trixie, it represented a moment of peace and a chance to know Vince better. Most of the time, they were alone in the apartment, but occasionally, like today, the crew was present.

"You smoke weed?" asked Vince taking a long pull.

"Nah, that stuff stinks," said Trixie.

"Try it, you look like you need to chill out," said Vince passing the blunt.

"Vince don't waste it. She doesn't know what she's doing. She just gonna get it wet," said Missy. Trixie puckered her lips, seductively, "Show me how to do it, boo."

"Trixie, you down with us now?" said one of Vince's blood brothers.

"I guess."

"Well, let's see what Ms. Trixie's working with," said Missy.

Missy was a tagalong. Heavyset and big breasted with short curly hair, she worked hard to keep the attention on her. Wherever the crew went, she was right there. They fought; she fought. She also kept the girls, who were always around, in check. While she hadn't slept with all the members, she wasn't committed to just one either, so when the crew needed a few extra dollars, she entertained older men to get what they needed. She wasn't pretty. In fact, she thought she was ugly, but her tight, low-cut tops and soft hair still drew attention. She was like the housemother. She made sandwiches for the boys and cleaned the place so they would keep her around. She had a room at home furnished with all the basics, including her mom's husband, who kept finding his way to her bedroom.

"What is that supposed to mean?" asked Trixie.

"Y'all stop. She's just kicking it with us until she gets her family stuff together," said Vince trying to get Trixie's attention.

"No, you stop it. You already violating by bringing a nobody in our spot. She wanna be down, then let her," said Missy spreading a blanket over the floor. Trixie braced up to Missy, ready to fight.

"I am down. I ain't a nobody." Hearing the commotion in the living room, several gang members and their girlfriends entered from the kitchen.

"Trixie wants to be a millionaire y'all. Grab a seat. This should be entertaining," said Missy.

"Nah," said Vince pulling Trixie toward the door.

"I'm down; who I got to fight?" Missy and her girls started laughing at Trixie.

"You got it all wrong, Ms. Magnet School. This is the new style initiation, and you got to do a 3.5. That means sleeping with our top three leaders for five minutes each, now drop them draws," said Missy.

The room grew quiet as everyone waited for Trixie to respond. Trixie stood, staring at an imaginary spot on the wall as her stomach clenched and rumbled. She struggled to believe that after all she'd done, her first time would be in a room full of strangers.

"I'm the leader of this group, and nobody gets this body again but me," said Vince.

Again!" Missy lunged at Trixie only to end up with a fist full of her braids in Trixie's hand.

"Don't run up on me like that. I am not the one," Trixie said, yanking Missy's head for emphasis.

"Let her go. Since Trixie is my woman, she can join us by taking the challenges," said Vince.

"Well, I get to decide one of her tasks," said Missy as her friend helped straighten her hair.

"Everybody out. It's late, and I need my rest," said Vince holding Trixie by the waist.

"Well, I'm taking the sofa," said Missy. "You and your girl can share the bed-again."

Trixie flopped onto her left side and tried to get comfortable. Sleep wasn't easy on the lumpy mattress in Vince's room. She missed her queen size bed and her flat screen. She also wasn't used to sleeping in a room with a boy even though Vince made a pallet on the floor. Secretly she yearned for her mother and the closeness she thought they were building, but she did not think she could return home soon. Maybe she should go live with Lawrence and Awana. If nothing else, that would hurt her mother.

Trixie pulled the photo album she borrowed from her mother's closet from under her pillow. Inside were pictures of her mother when she was younger. *Man, she was pretty*, Trixie thought as she flipped through each picture. Inside she saw images labeled Family Reunion; Mom, Dad, High School Prom; First Crush, and Me. There was also a picture of Tonya and Lawrence hugged up at a football game. The last picture was of her mom smiling and holding her as a baby.

"We have so much to lose," said Trixie as she kneeled to pray. Hours later, Trixie woke to cold water thrown on her. She must have fallen asleep on her knees.

"It's too late for prayer now," laughed Missy and her friend Rockelle.

"You want some more of this?" asked Trixie looking around for Vince. Folded at the bottom of the bed was the pallet where he slept. The right side of the bed looked slept in.

"Where's Vince?" asked Trixie.

"At my house. We are having a little pre-celebration for you."

"He wouldn't leave me here."

Missy tossed Trixie's shoes at her feet. "You got five minutes to meet me downstairs, or I'm driving off in your whip."

"Give me my keys." Rockelle stepped between Missy and Trixie. "You wanna be one of us, right? Ain't nobody gonna hurt your precious Beemer, stupid," said Rockelle. Trixie pulled on her shoes and followed Missy and Rockelle out the front door.

When Missy pulled in front of her house, she smiled at the number of teenagers standing around smoking and drinking. The bass from the music was so loud Trixie could barely hear herself think.

"I'm driving next," said Rockelle.

"Give me my keys," said Trixie holding out her hand to Missy. Trixie had never been in a fight, but she was ready.

"Thank you for letting me drive. Come inside, let's

party," said Missy. Trixie trailed behind Missy and Rockelle, dodging a guy who attempted to grab her hand.

"Your parents let you throw a party like this?"

"They gone for the week."

The teenagers crowded in Missy's living room were smoking weed or vaping. A cute dude with chocolate skin walked up to Trixie and handed her a cup. She looked around and saw Missy and Rockelle on the other side of the room. Trixie took a small sip of the drink. The dude smiled and opened his hand, pointing to a few brightly colored pills.

"Get out of my girl's face," said Vince taking the cup from Trixie and passing it back to the dude. Vince pulled Trixie down the hall, brushing off the girls who tried to get his attention.

"You left me," yelled Trixie over the music.

"Yet, you still here."

"Missy and Rockelle told me you wanted me to meet you here." Vince swore and dragged Trixie into one of the bedrooms.

"I was coming right back. They must have snuck out the house while I wasn't looking."

Trixie plopped down on the edge of the bed, "I should have known Missy was lying. Why do you even hang with her?"

"We family. Look, let's chill in here for a minute, and then we'll leave. This is not your type of party, and I don't want you out there." Trixie walked towards the dresser and picked up a pack of playing cards.

"Wanna play?"

"Strip poker?" asked Vince.

"You wish." Vince and Trixie settled onto the bed to play a few rounds of cards when the door burst open.

"Where is Missy?" Missy's stepfather Chris stood in the door glaring at Vince and Trixie. He was slim, high yellow, and dressed in starched jeans, a button-down shirt, and cowboy boots. His Cool Water cologne overpowered the space.

"What are you doing in her room?" asked Vince blocking Trixie from his view.

"Nigga, this my house. I should call the cops. Y'all underage drinking and stuff."

"Call the cops. I can call them on you too." Chris and Vince stared at each other.

"Tell Missy nobody better steal anything, and this place better be clean when me and her momma get back. Her momma got called into work, so we didn't go nowhere." Chris stared at Vince a few more seconds then left the room. Vince followed him and watched as he went out the back door.

"Stay here and lock the door. I'll be right back." A few moments later, Vince knocked on the door, "It's me."

Trixie opened the door, and Vince came in, followed by Missy.

"Is he gone?" asked Missy flustered.

"Man shut this party down, and let's go back to the apartment," said Vince.

"They in here!" Rockelle burst into the room as people gathered in the hallway outside the door.

Vince was the only person who knew about Missy's stepfather. She looked at Vince, begging him with her eyes to keep quiet.

"So, this is where the lames hang," said Missy as everyone started laughing.

Vince walked over to Missy, and Rockelle moved next to Trixie.

"I'll help you clean," said Vince.

"What are you talking about? We're gonna clean tomorrow. This is our party, and you letting her make you miss it," said Rockelle.

"How you gonna let your woman run things," said a voice out in the hall.

Trixie stood up, "Why y'all in our business?"

"Cause you in my room," said Missy.

"Y'all should be dancing and getting y'all drink on, but you two all caked up in my girl room. You remember this room, don't you, Vince," said Rockelle laughing.

Trixie glanced back at the bed in the room and then at Missy, who had a satisfied grin on her face. Trixie pushed past Missy, "Move."

Vince tried to keep Missy from leaving so he could convince her to stop the party, but she ignored him and left.

Back in the living room, the party had changed to a more serious vibe. Smoke thickened the air, and alcohol flowed around the room. Trixie grabbed a cup from the table and started drinking the contents.

"You don't know what's in that," yelled Vince attempting to take the cup.

"I'm not stupid. Stop treating me like a baby," said Trixie as she stomped off to sit on the sofa next to a girl sitting on a boy's lap. Trixie didn't want to look too closely, but the boy's hand was under her skirt as she swayed to the beat of the song. Trixie took another sip of her drink when she felt a hand on her shoulder. She ignored the hand thinking it was Vince trying to get her attention. Another tap. She looked over her shoulder and the guy from earlier was holding a drink in his hand for her.

"No pills," said Trixie. The guy pulled out a travel-size bottle of liquor and twisted the top. He poured it in the cup and shoved it towards Trixie. Trixie sniffed the drink and then mixed it with the punch in her cup.

"Let's dance," she said. Trixie was not the best dancer,

but she couldn't let Missy, who was bent over rubbing her butt on some dude's crotch outshine her.

Several drinks later, Trixie was having a blast sandwiched between several dudes. One of them attempted to stick his hands under her shirt when Vince shoved him to the side.

"Let's go."

"No," slurred Trixie. Vince attempted to pull Trixie out of the house. Trixie swung at him and fell to the floor.

"Trixie go lie in my room," said Missy.

"I'm good," said Trixie rolling over on her hands and knees. Missy grabbed her by the arm and shoved her towards the back of the house.

"Go to my room, or you won't be ready for tomorrow." Trixie nodded her head and stumbled towards the back of the room. Vince attempted to follow her.

"Let her go, boo. Ain't nobody gonna mess with her. We know she yo' girl," said Missy.

Trixie walked into Missy's room then turned around looking for the bathroom. She entered another room at the back of the house. The room was cream and black with a huge four-poster bed in the center. Black erotica was on the walls, used ashtrays, and partially burned incense sticks lay on the table next to the bed. Hot, Trixie pulled her shirt over her head, wiped the sweat on her forehead and between her breasts, then stretched out across the bed.

The party raged on in the other room, and soon Vince forgot about Trixie. No one saw Chris enter the house from the back door and walk into his room.

"Damn," said Chris when he saw Trixie lying on the bed. He fished his cell phone out of his pocket to call Missy's mother but slammed the phone on the nightstand and grabbed a blanket out of the closet instead. He threw it over Trixie then walked to lock the door.

"This my house," he grumbled, tugging off his boots and

shucking his pants around his ankle. Dressed only in a wife-beater and boxers, he stood staring at Trixie. He ran a finger along her cheek, lifted the blanket, and traced the curve of her spine. He took a few pictures of her sleeping then slid under the blanket and wrapped an arm around her.

***

"Meet me at the mall for three," said Missy slamming the front door in Trixie's face. Thirty minutes later, Trixie opened the door to Vince's apartment so she could shower and sleep a few more hours before meeting the crew. Her head felt heavy, and her mouth had a foul taste to it. She wished Vince was with her so he could tell her what happened at the party, but him and his boys were probably still asleep at Missy's house.

Last night when she woke up in Missy's mother's bed, she panicked and stumbled into the living room. Vince and his boys were around the room sleeping on the floor and sofa, while Rockelle and Missy were cleaning. Tonya never spoke to Trixie about drugs and drinking. Still, she knew her behavior could have gotten her in serious trouble.

In the bathroom, Trixie grabbed three aspirin from the cabinet and took several gulps of the warm water streaming from the faucet. She walked back into Vince's room and curled under the cover.

The Willowbrook area in North Houston was a popular spot for all ages. Littered with restaurants, family joints, and a few things for the grown and sexy, the mall sat at a busy intersection. Trixie parked her SUV and climbed in the back seat of Vince's brother's car.

"So, what's the assignment? Let's do this," said Trixie.

"You can't be ready in those high heels," mocked Missy.

"Don't hate. These Gucci boo."

"Well, I hope you can run in Gucci cause assignment one is to steal something over one hundred dollars," said Rockelle from the front seat.

"Y'all said nothing about stealing. I thought I would pull a prank or something," said Trixie.

"Well, surprise. You've got thirty minutes to get the stuff and meet us at entrance five. If you're late, we're gone. Rockelle is going to be your shadow to make sure you do it right," said Missy.

Trixie turned to Rockelle, "So how do I do this? Do I put it in my clothes?"

"Look, I ain't your friend, just do it and you better hurry," said Rockelle heading into the store.

Rockelle was slim and brown skinned with a waist length weave. She dreamed of being a model even though people told her she was too short. She loved being creative. She took pride in trying out different looks from stores like Family Dollar and Rainbow. Her mother had four younger children, so she spent most of her attention on them while Rockelle was left to fend for herself making money selling gummies and other edibles to the kids at school and in the neighborhood. One day she wanted to live in LA and dress celebrities for music videos. A lot of them were her friends on social media so she figured it was only a matter of time before she got her big break.

Rockelle stood a few feet from Trixie looking for a designer shirt she could wear with her knock off jeans. Trixie headed to the Jr's section when a voice startled her.

"Hey, cutie, can I help you with anything?" asked the salesclerk.

Bingo thought Trixie as she stared at a chunky teen + with a bad case of acne.

"I was looking for something for my big brother until I saw you. What's up?" asked Trixie walking closer.

The salesclerk pointed at Rockelle, "Is that girl over there with you?"

"Uh yea, she's just a friend," said Trixie walking away.

"Wait, don't go, I know what this is. She used to make runs with a boy from my crew. How much you need?"

"You don't know me," said Trixie.

"How much you got to steal to get in. You tryna roll, right?"

"Huh?"

"Look, I'll let you have this tracksuit for ninety and your phone number."

"All I got is fifty," bartered Trixie.

"You tripping. This is a 200.00 deal. I'll even put it in a bag for you." Trixie thought about how easy it would be to use some of her money to complete task one.

"If you take 85.00, we got a deal," said Trixie scribbling her cell number on a piece of paper.

"Drop the money on the floor and take the suit to the dressing room. There should be some shopping bags in the corner." Trixie dropped the money on the floor and headed to get a shopping bag. When she left the dressing room, Rockelle was not in sight. As she wandered toward the exit door, she thought about how simple task one had been.

"Excuse me sir, can you take off my tags, Trixie said as the alarm started blaring. She turned to see the salesclerk who helped her earlier and smiled. She walked towards him, but he grabbed her by the arm and started dragging her away from the exit.

"Security, security," he yelled.

"Wait, what are you doing, I thought we had a deal," whispered Trixie.

"Remember the guy on the city bus? He was my cousin. Guess you didn't see me waiting for him at the corner when you jumped off. The cops had to be called and everything," he said, jerking Trixie's arm.

"I'm sorry it was just a joke."

"Well, payback is a mutha-" Trixie raked her nails across his face and scrambled out the door. When she made it to the pickup spot, she saw Vince and his crew leaving the mall.

***

I felt my blood pressure rise as I paced the floor of Tonya's home. I was so upset it didn't matter that I was in the same room with my wife and my first love.

"What do you mean you don't know where your daughter is?" I asked.

"If you holler at me one more time, it's on. What I want to know is what you did to my baby while you and your wife were having dinner with her?"

I saw Awana flinch then relax. From the moment we arrived, I sensed she was trying to be objective and not feel jealous that Tonya was Trixie's mother, but I knew my wife, and she was not going to take being insulted much longer.

"I think everyone needs to calm down. Tonya have you and Trixie had any arguments lately?" asked Awana.

"What's that supposed to mean. Trixie and I have been doing fine. This all started after her dinner with you y'all," said Tonya pointing her finger.

"My daughter and me had a good time. She said you two were trying to salvage your relationship. I knew I should have pressed harder to get her away from you," I said.

"Don't tell me you brought up a custody battle. Trixie is not three. She is almost sixteen. She can tell the judge who she wants to live with. She barely knows you," said Tonya.

"That's my point. Once the judge learns about Trixie's

exploits and your promiscuity, no one will dispute Awana and I are the better parents."

"Get out of my house. You will never have my daughter. Never. Both of you think you can turn her against me, but I have news for you. You keep messing with me, and you will end up floating in the bayou," said Tonya. I watched as Tonya walked to the bookshelf and thumbed through her collection.

"What are you looking for? The number to the criminals in your family? No one is afraid of them. I have connections too. We are from the same hood. You mess with me, and there will be no need for a custody hearing."

Tonya walked towards me then stopped an arm's length away, "No court will award custody to a man who has a taste for young girls. In fact, right after we broke up, I heard you got a fourteen-year-old pregnant." I lunged at Tonya and closed my hands around her throat. Calling me a pedophile was a low blow. Not even Awana knew how traumatic it was when a family friend accused my father of molestation. Thankfully, the truth came out, but my parent's marriage barely survived. My siblings and I were bullied so badly we had to switch schools and attend counseling.

"Lying slut, don't make up lies to further your case."

"Like father, like son," said Tonya.

"My father was innocent, and you know it. I would never do something like that."

"Go ahead, bruise me up."

Tonya squealed as if I were applying pressure to her throat. This was my first time putting a hand on a woman, and I had no idea what Awana's reaction would be. "Stop it both of you!" Awana pummeled my back and yanked my arm.

"How long has Lawrence been beating you? Have you

tried to get help? Are you afraid for your life?" asked Tonya rubbing her throat.

"He does not abuse me," said Awana standing between Tonya and me.

"Give it up, Tonya. You know I am not abusive, nor am I a pedophile. I was not applying pressure to your throat. You're venomous, and the sooner I get Trixie away from you, the better."

"Putting a hand on a woman is never right even if you weren't choking her. I don't like the way you've been handling things." Awana walked away from me and picked up her purse.

"Baby, please. Let me explain. I've been so stressed."

"That's no excuse," said Tonya. I regretted putting my hands on her, but I did not want to apologize.

"Listen, what I did was wrong pleas-" Tonya turned away from me and dropped her head. She refused to look at me.

"It's late. Let's get a fresh perspective in the morning. I'll ask some of Trixie's friends at the youth center if they know where she is," said Awana.

"Fine, I'll be there at nine," said Tonya, still not facing us.

"Since when do you even turn over before noon," I scoffed.

"Please, you know better. That's you after running through half the campus in college," said Tonya.

"At least I didn't start in my teens."

"I'm a mother intent on protecting her child. You haven't seen the lengths I will go."

"Tonya, Lawrence and I are not trying to take Trixie from you. I believe she needs you, but you also need to understand how hard it is for a man who wants to be a father having his rights denied." Tonya walked back to the book-shelf. She kept her face away from Awana and me.

"I'm not trying to deny him. But he has no right to come in here-"

Tonya went silent. I saw her take several breaths, heard the tears in her voice. The doorbell saved me from experiencing sympathy I didn't want to feel. I knew she loved Trixie. She was also caring and thoughtful by nature even though few people saw that side of her. Many years ago, I was one of those people. Now, she was my enemy. She could save her tears.

"I'll get the door, I'm sure it's Vince." I disliked him on sight. He looked like a typical street thug who lied with every breath. If I found out he was messing with my baby girl, I'm doing life, gladly. Before anyone could say a word to him, I shoved him down the hall.

"I need to talk to you privately, man to man," I said in a calm voice. Vince walked ahead of me into Tonya's room. I turned the lock, then slammed him into the opposite wall. Awana and Tonya banged on the bedroom door.

Vince eyed me for a moment then pushed away from the wall. "We good," he hollered to Awana and Tonya.

"If you're sleeping with my daughter, I'll tear you apart."

"Go ahead. I'm not telling you where she is. She deserves better than you and Ms. Tonya." The plan was to rough him up a bit and threaten him with a couple of street thugs, but days of anxiety and exhaustion hit home quickly. Jumbo tears rolled down my face, and I slumped onto the edge of Tonya's bed. Vince shook his head at me and walked out of the room. I could hear him talking to Tonya.

"Maybe she's better off with none of y'all," said Vince.

"2341 MLK-"

"What kind of game are you playing?" asked Vince. I considered going into the living room, but I didn't think my legs would hold my weight.

"That's your momma's address. A little more digging and

I will know what she fixes your daddy for breakfast. Did you know he's cozy with the neighbor?" asked Tonya.

I gave a weak chuckle. *That's the girl I know. Anything to get our baby back.* I forgot just how dirty Tonya could play when her back was against the wall. I may not have as much money as her, but I was desperate, and desperate people do not have a conscience. I settled back into the chair to listen at how this would play out.

EPISODE FOUR

ONE HOT MOMMA

4,320 minutes. 259, 200 seconds. My heart gone-missing.

"I will update the social media pages and sift through your inboxes. I told you not to post a reward. Half the messages I've been receiving are from people trying to con you out of money. Tonya? Hello?"

I hung up the phone on Valerie. She'd understand. I leaned over the edge of the bed and threw up clear bile. I had not eaten more than a piece of fruit the past few days. I wasn't hungry. I wasn't fasting. I was dying, slowly and painfully, every second my child was out of my sight. I collapsed onto the pillows and felt a cool towel caress my forehead.

"We should go," said Pastor Donnelly.

"It'll only make things worse."

"They are your family. You need them." I rolled onto my side and stared at Pastor Donnelly through puffy eyes. If the usher board at Guiding Light knew their pastor was in my bedroom I'd be banned for life. I didn't even want him here.

He was a decent man, never even tried to hold my hand. I knew he had a crush on me; women could sense these things. He would make some woman incredibly happy. It won't be me. I couldn't stand the sight of him. He represented the goodness I no longer had. I was at war.

"Let me get dressed." I watched Pastor Donnelly leave the room, barely refraining from rolling my eyes at him. I'd be glad when he went home. For now, he would be just what I needed as I visited my childhood home for the first time in almost sixteen years.

***

"Neighborhoods like this make me miss home," said Pastor Donnelly as he drove closer to my childhood home.

"You're not from Texas?" I asked, directing him to my mother's house. I didn't want to be here, but I'd do anything to find my child, and whether or not I liked it, the older residents of Sunnyside always had an ear to the ground.

"New Orleans, lots of family, fun, and good eating," said Pastor Donnelly.

"I've thought about visiting, but I'm more inclined to travel to places with a reputation for high
fashion.

"What about for the Essence Festival?"

"Black girl magic is not really my thing. Moving up in the finance world, I rarely met a black male, and most of the women were useless in the corporate arena. They spent most of their time trying to downplay what's between their legs, instead of bonding with the next sista."

Pastor Donnelly shook his head and opened the car door.

I walked up to the front door and rang the doorbell. My first shock came when my daddy answered. My next shock was the living space. This was not my childhood home. The threadbare carpet had been replaced with hardwood floors and the walls were a warm gold.

"Your momma will be out in a sec," said my father.

"Ok." I did not know what else to say. My daddy was the center of my universe. Growing up, I didn't think twice about requesting an expensive pair of shoes or my weekly trips to the beauty salon. When he left me, I tried to keep myself pretty for him. I figured at some point he'd come back for me, and I wanted him to be proud.

"My eyes darn near popped out of my head when I saw you at the door. It's really good to see you here looking so well." My dad attempted to embrace me, but I walked a few steps away to keep from throwing myself in his arms.

"Have you been taking care of yourself ? Where have you been living?" I asked.

"Slow down Tonya, you never gave a person a chance to answer one question before you shot off another one," said my mom entering the room. I half rolled my eyes before turning to face her.

"Momma?" She looked different, in a good way.

"Hey Tonya. You look good." Instead of walking into her embrace, I stood stiffly in the corner with my hands clasped in front of me.

"Mrs. Peterson, nice to meet you. I'm Pastor Donnelly."

"She's not a Mrs. anymore. Didn't you go back to your maiden name after my daddy got his freedom?" Everyone was quiet for a few seconds before my mom chuckled and pulled me into her arms.

"You're look fantastic baby. I know you hate me, but I'm your mother, and I love you." I cleared my throat as if it were itching.

"Dad, I'm glad you're here. I don't want to inconvenience you two but-"

"My wife is not an inconvenience."

"Come on, somebody," said Pastor Donnelly from the corner.

Jesus, be a fence. At least bring me some patience. I eyed my daddy in his creased khakis and button-down shirt. His shoes had the same shine from when I was a little girl. He looked a little skinny, but he appeared healthy.

"Daddy, I know you mean well, but you two were divorced. I didn't want to burden anyone with my problems," I said. My mom walked over to me and grabbed my hands.

"You will never be a burden to me. Your daddy and I got each other, and we want to be there for you."

"Got each other?" My daddy put his arm around my mom's shoulder, "We never got divorced," he said.

I looked at the two of them for a moment, and then started walking towards the front door. I would rather find Trixie on my own than deal with the two of them.

"Tonya, wait, let your parents explain, said Pastor Donnelly grabbing my hand.

"This has nothing to do with you. Stay out of it." I took a seat on the sofa, placing my purse next to me. I needed space.

"Tonya don't talk to a man of God like that," my mom said.

"Right, I forgot how sanctified you are."

"Now you listen to me, Tonya. I coddled you too much. Your mom worked hard to change. Look at this house and the flat screen. Theresa sits righte next to my beer and my chips when the game is on, sorry Rev."

"I enjoy a good game too, minus the beer," said Pastor Donnelly with a chuckle.

If our biggest issue as a family was a beer on game days, this would be a breeze, but it was not. My childhood was shortened because my mom ran my dad away. I hate to admit it, but my father let her. He could have pushed harder to see me. Even when I became an adult, he stayed away. The men in my life could win awards for abandoning me. I never wanted my child to feel insignificant and unworthy because her father wasn't present. I tried to fill a void no woman can fill. I messed up. Trixie's disappearance, the boys, everything was my fault.

"Tonya, don't you notice something different about your momma?" My daddy stepped closer to mom and wrapped his arms around her. She leaned back against his chest. I felt like my head would explode. I looked at my mother closely. She sported a pair of bootcut jeans, a printed t-shirt, and a short haircut to complement her round face.

"Ma, where did you get those pants and who cut your hair."

"Delores' girl takes me shopping on Saturdays. In exchange, I let her experiment on my hair since she's in beauty school. She okay, but if she messes it up, I use my clip-on tracks."

"Clip-on tracks! No, ma'am. My stylist will take care of your hair."

"Yep baby, things have changed for the better. I just wish you could have been a part of it all," said Theresa.

"Why didn't someone call me?"

"How?" asked Theresa,

"You have a non-published number," my daddy said. Growing up, he rarely fussed at me, but when he did, I became a water pot. I felt like one now.

"You sent cards."

"And you probably didn't open them. All we could do was trust God," said my mother.

"Well, I think now is the right time for prayer," said Pastor Donnelly.

"Wait! I came here about Trixie. Momma, daddy, I need you to help find my baby."

My dad looked at me, and shook his head, "She's all right."

"She's not all right! I haven't seen her in almost a week. The police are no help. She could be dead."

"Tonya, calm down. Valerie called us when she learned Trixie was missing. She's ok." I slammed my purse down on the coffee table. "What do you mean, she's ok? You've known all this time where my daughter was, and you let me suffer?"

"Tonya, let me explain," my dad said.

"You don't have a right to explain anything to me. You left me. You stopped being a daddy to me the minute you stopped being her wife. But then you came back for her and not me."

"I'm sorry, baby girl. I have a lot to atone for. I allowed your momma to take a lot of the blame for our hard life, but the truth is I wasn't innocent. Let's talk about this.

"Where is my child? Tell me now, or I'm calling the police."

"I don't know the address, but several people saw her riding in the car you brought her. I gave the boy she's been staying with my number, and she called me earlier today. I knew you'd eventually come to me for help. I'm sorry, but I wanted to see you so badly. I was gonna tell you she was ok if I hadn't spoken to you by this evening."

"Just tell me where she is, or I will find out myself. I knew she was with Vince."

My momma grabbed me by the hands. "Baby, she's not ready to come home, but I will try to convince her."

I jerked my hands away, "What do you mean? That's my child."

My dad rubbed my shoulder. "Let us help you. It will be ok. Your momma and I will call you when she gets here. If she isn't here before nightfall, I will get her myself. I promise."

My mom hugged me tightly, "Please let us make this right. We have so much to atone for. I love you, Tonya." For the first time in my life, I cried in my mother's arms. They felt like home.

EPISODE FIVE

BLACK MAN OUT

This is my final bow. My run is over. To them, I'm insignificant. It took me three hours and four substations to realize the police protected their own and served only themselves.

"When I get home, I'm going to make more calls and reach out to Tonya. I can't believe Trixie is still missing," said Awana. I stalked to the car, not bothering to open her door. Awana and I rode in silence for the next thirty minutes. I wasn't able to have a civil conversation. Instead, I settled for gunning my car through the city streets and turning corners like a lunatic.

"I'm sorry if it feels like I'm not supportive, but I love you, and I want this to work out. I can't believe the police wouldn't help us. Once we find Trixie, I think we should speak with Tonya about letting her live with us for the summer. Then Trixie can see what life will be like with us and decide to stay," said Awana.

"Get out." I brought the car to a stop and unbuckled her seatbelt.

"Excuse me," said Awana.

"I'm moving out. Once the custody hearing is final, I'll be getting a divorce," I told Awana.

"Divorce!"

"You don't want my daughter. You don't want me."

"I'm trying to help you. I've testified in custody cases before. Your case is weak. I don't want you to damage your chances of being a father to Trixie. Why can't you understand that?" pleaded Awana.

"You need to decide if you're for me or against me. I'll come for my clothes later." I waited for her to exit. I didn't want a divorce, but I needed people on my team to support me one hundred percent.

"You better get them before I pull a *Waiting to Exhale.* Divorce me now because you won't use me to get custody then drop me when you feel you don't need me to put up a front any longer," said Awana stepping out the car.

I backed down the driveway, drove a few blocks then pulled on the side of a dumpster behind a local grocery store. I gripped the steering wheel then pounded out my frustration- left, right, left, right, until my hands throbbed, and sharp pain radiated up my arm. My head bounced off the head rest, repeatedly. I yelled until my voice grew hoarse. Snot and tears leaked down my face. My chest hurt. My heart was broken. I snatched up the business card from the detective at the local precinct and ripped it to shreds. What a joke! Since I wasn't on Trixie's birth certificate the police wouldn't give me any information. They wouldn't even tell me if Tonya filed a missing person's report. They treated me like the black man I was. Never mind, I was successful and degreed with no record, trying to be a decent father. Like so many men before me, the system ignored my right to love and protect my child. I was silenced, permanently terminated as a father, and I still didn't know where to find my daughter.

***

Trixie sat Indian style on her bed, gnawing at her nails. She needed to bail, but she had nowhere to go. After escaping the mall, Trixie waited down the street from her house for an hour, afraid the police were waiting to arrest her. At her wit's end, she finally called Vince. If nothing else, she would get some relief from giving him his walking papers.

"Hey Vince, this is Trixie."

"I see you made it home okay."

"No thanks to you; you set me up," Trixie yelled.

"Nobody set you up," said Vince getting louder.

"Whatever, just tell me what happened after everybody left me."

"Rockelle told us you chickened out and left her in the store."

"Man, when I see her again, I'mma show her," said Trixie.

"That won't happen, you out."

"But why, I did what I was supposed to do."

"Look, this life is not for you. I took your charge, and they jumped you out."

"You didn't get hurt too badly, did you?"

"Nah, them fools know better."

"I've got to get outta here. It feels like the walls are closing in on me," said Trixie.

"You can always come back over here. I'm taking a break from the crew. Things are getting a little tired, know what I'm saying."

"You can do that?"

"Not really, but half of them wanna be number one, so they not tripping."

"Y'all fake anyway. Ain't even hard."

"Girl stop playing. You don't want this smoke."

"I guess. I'm on my way, but first, I need to expose the enemy."

Tuesday night Bible study was a time where the members of Guiding Light experienced their pastor and the word of God in a more intimate setting. Although members at the southwest location numbered close to 1,500, evening services barely topped fifty since most members felt one day a week with Jesus was enough. Trixie entered from the back of the sanctuary and took a seat on the last pew. Pastor Donnelly was standing in front of the first row.

"You've been a faithful member for 15 years now, Sister Smith. What has kept you here for so long?" asked Pastor Donnelly.

"The genuine love you have for people. Throughout the bible, Jesus mandates that we show love. As my pastor, you've exemplified this principle."

"Thank you for that, Sister. Who can find a scripture about love?" asked Pastor Donnelly.

A middle-aged man raised his hand. "What about John 15:13 'Greater love has no one than this that he lay down his life for his friends.'"

Pastor Donnelly shook his head, "That's a wonderful example. Anybody else?"

Trixie stood up and walked down the center aisle, "I have a question."

Tonya turned around and ran to hug Trixie. She didn't want everyone to know their business, but she latched onto Trixie's waist and clasped her tightly. She could barely contain her relief.

"Exodus reminds children to honor their parents. Isn't that one form of love?" asked Trixie hugging Tonya.

"It sure is. Love and honor are qualities that Christians

should extend to all people. That's good. How about one more example?" said Pastor Donnelly.

"Pastor. surely God understands how hard it is to love a parent who didn't want you to begin with and uses men for money, including men of the cloth." Tonya detangled herself from Trixie.

"Trixie, what's wrong with you?" asked Tonya.

"Or how about loving a mother who wished she would have aborted me? You can't deny it, mother, I heard it with my own ears," said Trixie. The members gasped and shook their heads. Several women eyed each other. Pastor Donnelly walked towards Trixie.

"I think you may have misunderstood some things," said Pastor Donnelly putting his hand on Trixie's shoulder.

"You make me sick. You're the one she was talking to. You a hypocrite. Why not tell the church how you've been banging my momma?" One of the church mothers stood and walked towards Trixie. Pastor Donnelly held up a hand for silence.

"Tiffany Peterson stop it. If you have something against me, take it up with me," said Tonya.

"So now I'm Tiffany? Please. I'm done here," said Trixie. Tonya raced behind Trixie.

"I can't believe you waltzed into the house of the Lord with mess and confusion. When we get home, you and I have some serious issues to discuss."

"I'm not going to your house, mother. I'm going to be with my man. It's about time I made use of the birth control you make me take." Tonya charged Trixie and grabbed her by the hair. Pastor Donnelly and a deacon worked to break them apart.

"I hate you," screamed Trixie as she ran out of the church.

***

"So, she kicked Missy out the house?" asked Trixie.

"Yep, she chose her man over her daughter," said Vince.

"Man, I thought I had it bad," said Trixie.

"You have it bad because that's how you make it. Your momma gives you everything you need. You don't have to hustle to eat," said Vince.

"No, but that's nothing. She does that because she knows she has to. She doesn't love me though.

"Love? This ain't Cosby. This is ghetto love. My boy's mom puts a lock on the refrigerator. He keeps an ice chest in his room. He's only fourteen but pays part of the rent with his hustle money."

"Do you sell drugs," asked Trixie.

"I do what I have to when I have to."

"What does that mean because I might not be perfect, but I'm not into drugs," said Trixie.

"It means what I'm doing right now, is not what I plan on doing ten years from now. I want an auto body shop. I took some classes at school, and sometimes I hang out with my partner Hugo. His dad has his own business."

"Why did you quit school?" asked Trixie.

"I didn't quit. I mean, a brother isn't dumb. I just don't have time for people telling me what to do. Those teachers are fake anyway. They do more dirt than the kids."

"That's true," said Trixie.

"Why were you in counseling?" asked Vince. Trixie sat on the couch contemplating how much to share. Vince knew a lot about street life, but she didn't want him to label her as trash.

"Come on, spill the beans. What was it? Fighting, cussing out the teacher?" said Vince jokingly.

"Something like that," said Trixie.

"Are you going to keep secrets after I told you all my business? I got a little cousin who is selfish like you."

"You don't know me," said Trixie.

"Rich, pretty, stable home life, but don't appreciate it."

"I guess."

"Your mom is like every other mom at my school. They think because the school isn't calling home every day, it's all good. Some of the smartest kids be the biggest freaks and hustlers," said Vince shaking his head.

"For real," said Trixie thinking of her own situation.

"Trixie, you got to go home," said Vince.

"What you mean, I thought you said I could stay here."

"Look you rolling with me now, and you can't be disrespecting yourself. I know stuff is deep with your mom, but this life isn't for you. If you don't get out now, you might get lost to the streets. Go on home and work it out," said Vince pulling Trixie towards the front door.

Trixie parked her car outside the garage and hit the alarm. She was sure Tonya heard her drive up, but she wanted to give her extra notice.

"You are the baby's daddy," reported Maury from the 70-inch screen. Tonya lay on the couch, staring at her and Trixie's favorite afternoon show. She had just finished praying for the tenth time that day when Trixie walked into the room.

"Momma, I'm sorry." Tonya stood and faced Trixie.

"No, Trixie, it's me. I've been a horrible parent. I prayed-" Tonya and Trixie tried to speak at the same time.

"Seniority rules," said Trixie jokingly.

"Watch it, I'm still cute. I was so worried when you stormed out the church. I've been doing a lot of praying.

"I can tell, there wasn't anything flying at my head when I walked in."

"I should have shared my life with you. I shouldn't have

kept you from my family. I almost let my bitterness destroy us."

"We have time momma," said Trixie.

"I never wanted an abortion, Trixie."

"Momma, it's okay." Trixie pulled Tonya down onto the sofa. "I said we have time. This is the best part. I bet he's not the daddy," said Trixie as she placed her head on her mother's shoulder.

Two weeks later, Tonya and Trixie's relationship continued to flourish. They stayed up late into the night with girl talk. Tonya even made sure she was awake before Trixie left for school in the morning. Although Tonya hadn't spoken to her parents since their shaky reunion, she believed in her heart a full reconciliation was a part of their future. Trixie had not been in touch with her father since the day she stormed out of Awana's office, but she emailed Awana with updates on her counseling session with her new therapist.

"Come on mom, why can't I go this once?" whined Trixie.

"Because I don't know him. I don't see why you two can't study over here," said Tonya.

"Please tell me you're kidding. I don't need constant supervision. Couldn't you have tried to parent me when I was like ten?" said Trixie eyeing her mother.

"Trixie, I won't make excuses or let past failures dictate my future responsibilities. Now you can either help him study over here, or he's on his own." *I don't like this parenting thing very much,* thought Tonya as she waited for Trixie's response.

"You did marvelous ole girl. I guess my friend and I will study in the kitchen," said Trixie with a cheeky. Trixie walked out of her bedroom and back into the kitchen where Vince sat at the table struggling with a math equation.

"Man, if this is the stuff I can expect on the GED test, I can forget it," said Vince taking a sip of soda.

"Why don't you finish high school," said Tonya sitting at the table. Trixie gave her mother the evil eye, which Tonya ignored as she chomped on a pretzel.

"I don't have the patience," said Vince.

"Well, I admire your determination. You just need help on your math skills." Tonya pulled the notebook towards her and solved the problem.

"You did that fast," said Trixie.

"Numbers baby, I'm good with anything dealing with numbers. You know I gets my bag, ya heard me."

"Oh, my god. Let's go chill in my room," said Trixie grabbing Vince's hand.

"Uh, Trixie." Tonya paused for a second to gather the words to sound like a mother but not embarrass Trixie.

"I already told you I don't want, uhm, boys in this house. I mean, it's okay in this house, but not in your room," said Tonya.

"You know what mom, you really make me- gotcha," yelled Trixie.

"Why you little brat, you gon' pay for that girl."

"Excuse me, Mrs. Peterson, but it's you are going to pay for that," said Vince as he started laughing.

"Whew," said Trixie trying to recover. "The look on your face."

Priceless, just like this moment, thought Tonya as she and Trixie shared knowing looks.

EPISODE SIX

WE GOOD, SIS

I turned into the parking lot of a popular eatery on Houston's Northeast side and mentally cursed as I navigated my car over potholes filled with gravel. I suggested this place because I felt a bit nostalgic after seeing my parents for the first time in years, plus the rundown restaurant had delicious soul food and teacakes on the menu. Awana was probably trying to prover her blackness when she accepted my choice of restaurant, but it doesn't matter. I'm not trying to be her best friend. If I have to play nice to make sure she stays on my team, so be it.

"She all right," I mumbled as I watched Awana settle at the table. We engaged in chit chat for about ten minutes until I got tired of the strain and extended an olive branch.

"Thanks for inviting me to lunch. I can't believe Lawrence is divorcing you," I said sipping my lemonade.

"I received a certified letter today."

"He is being such an ass."

"Careful, I still love the man. How's Trixie?

"She's been back for two weeks, and I feel so fortunate."

"So, tell me what happened with Trixie's school counselor?" asked Awana. Mr. Clayton was still a sore subject for me. It hurt that my parenting was so horrible Trixie couldn't come to me about being assaulted. My mother had faults, a lot of them, but I knew if anyone ever tried to harm me, she was the person to tell. My dad would hold me and tell me I would be okay. Theresa Peterson, however, would rain up fire from hell. We had that in common. I was upset with my lawyer when he told me Mr. Clayton was secluded in a Mid-Town psych ward after he attempted to kidnap Trixie. I wanted him in a jail cell. He needed to learn to keep his hands to himself, and experience is always the best teacher. The local newspaper ran a front-page story detailing his twelve years in education and the ten plus unsubstantiated complaints of inappropriate relationships with students. The story also included the charges his mother filed on her best friend for starting a sexual relationship with him at fourteen.

"My lawyer told me the struggles he faced growing up. I don't give a damn."

"Me either. The school system needs to do a better job researching these people. He never reported half of the jobs he held."

"Well, at least he won't be bothering Trixie anymore. I thought I would have to call my cousin Pookie," said Tonya smacking her lips.

"Oh-kay," said Awana throwing up a high-five.

I high-fived Awana trying not to laugh. I was sure the only Pookies she knew were on the TV screen.

"So why don't you and Lawrence have children?" I asked after the server finished refilling my drink.

"I guess God had a better mother in mind. I've had five miscarriages."

"Or he chose a special lady like you to mother children who've lost their parents. Have you ever thought about adopting?"

"No, I just started accepting that I'll never have children of my own."

"Well, anything is possible. Look at the two of us breaking bread together. Are you sure you want to testify for me? It may mess up your chance at a reconciliation.

Awana sipped her Sprite and dabbed her mouth, "I'm not sure if it's the right thing to do as a wife, but you don't deserve to lose your daughter."

I squeezed Awana's hand, "Let's pray Lawrence comes around, and everyone survives the next couple of months," I said signaling for the check.

BLACK ON BLACK BUSINESS

Max poured a glass of whiskey, took one sip, and then another. At 6'5, most people assumed Max Evans was an athlete in college, then a coach when his career ended. He still got stares when he entered a room and the proverbial what position he played or what team he rooted for question. He didn't take offense since by American standards being a brown man in America came with a slew of stereotypes much worse than being an athlete. Carrying his drink, Max settled into his favorite chair.

"I need an injunction," said Lawrence coming out of the bathroom.

"Not possible."

"Will you put the liquor down? You will not get plastered on my dime."

"First, you're on my dime. Second, you've been going for almost two hours about this case. I need a drink."

Lawrence picked up his bag and walked towards the door, "I think I need to find another attorney to handle my hearing."

Max drained his glass and poured a splash more into his glass. "Call my assistant if you need a referral."

"You can't take this seriously because you don't have any kids or a wife." Lawrence sat on the sofa, placing his bag at his feet. "I'm losing everything!"

"Man listen, I didn't buy my degree, and I didn't get where I am by not taking my cases seriously. Sorry about the drinking. You don't need another lawyer. I got you."

"See, you're not being professional. If I were at a white law office, he wouldn't be saying 'I got you.'"

Max walked out of the living room and returned with a large stack of papers. He slammed them on the table in front of Lawrence.

"Open it."

Lawrence opened the folder, glanced at a few pages, and closed the file, "I don't know what I'm looking at."

"Because I am the lawyer. Now, I've already apologized for drinking on the clock, but I thought this would be an informal meeting where I would share with you what I've already put in motion."

Lawrence opened the folder. Max sat next to him.

"These are the motions I filed. The first one is to have our case looked at by a mediator."

"But I want my custody to be official," said Lawrence.

"It will be. I also petitioned for unsupervised visitation. Make sure you don't speak to anyone without me present. There may be reporters looking for a story."

"What does the media have to do with this? I'm a nobody."

"So is Tonya, but her lawyer isn't. With his reputation and the fact that Tonya has an open case with Trixie and her counselor getting publicity won't be hard.

"Make sure you hit that point in court and the fact that she messes with boys, just like her mother. Did you investigate her finances? I bet she slept her way into some of her biggest portfolios."

"Lawrence are you sure you want to go this deep? Tonya is smart. I traced her career, and she's legit."

Max scribbled some notes on the outside of the folder.

"I'm not surprised she's been successful, but I'd bet money she had no problem adding a little icing."

Max patted Lawrence on the back and poured him a drink, "I'll follow your lead. If I hit too hard, say the word."

Lawrence took a sip of his drink, "I'm sorry for what I said earlier. You have my permission to do whatever is necessary."

"Don't sweat it. You will get custody. Tonya isn't the only one who plays dirty."

***

Lawrence placed Trixie's suitcases on the full-size bed and nervously eyed the spare bedroom. This room was more than enough for the few visitors he and Awana had during their marriage. Now, when he needed to make a good impression on his teenage daughter, Lawrence saw the room as lacking amenities.

"Why don't you leave some of your things in the closet this time that way you don't have to keep packing and unpacking."

"It's fine."

"You wanna go to Home Depot and pick up some paint for the walls? You can change the room however you want," said Lawrence.

"It's fine, but this full-size bed has got to go. I had more room in my crib as a baby. I'm sporting a queen now, and my mother promised I could have a king size if I stayed at home for college," said Trixie.

Lawrence placed Trixie's suitcases on the side of her bed, "Your room must be huge. Tonya always liked the finer things, but I intend to bring a little order and balance to your life."

"Look, I understand where you're coming from, but I don't need you to repair whatever my mother may have done wrong in your eyes. I'm only here because you got visitation until the judge decides custody."

"Trixie, this is difficult for both of us, but I really think everything will work out for the best. Why don't you get settled and make a list of the things you need to make your room more personal while I get dinner ready?"

"You cook?"

"Any man that wanted to be with Awana had to cook, clean, and paint toenails," laughed Lawrence.

"This would be easier if she were here. Don't you miss her?"

Lawrence walked to Trixie's door, "Despite what may have happened between us, she loves you and is always available."

"Do you think the two of you will make up?"

"I'll get dinner ready before it gets late."

Lawrence left Trixie in her room, barely holding his emotions in check. Now was the time to focus on getting to know Trixie, not pining over his soon to be ex-wife; she made her choice. His first and only priority was having Trixie in his life, permanently.

Trixie opened her suitcase and pulled out some clothes to relax in. When she came for visits, she took out and put back what she needed daily, only placing her makeup on the dresser. She and her mother were doing better, and she didn't want to jinx anything by getting too comfortable. Trixie exited her room and went down the hall to the bathroom.

She hated not having one connected to her room. She heard her phone ring and ran to answer it.

"Hey."

"Hey." Trixie grabbed her phone and walked back to the bathroom.

"You made it to his house?"

"Uh, huh."

"When can I come and see you?" asked Vince.

Trixie placed the phone on mute and flushed the toilet, "I don't know. I doubt Lawrence will allow me to have company. He's ok on some things, but I'm scared to think about you coming over.

"So, how's your mom doing?"

"I don't want to talk about her. I just want to focus on the weekend going fast."

"You uncomfortable?"

"Not really, but it's not like I know him, know him."

"Well, next time you go I'mma come through. I need to see my girl."

***

Trixie and Tonya settled at the kitchen table with their attorney Christopher St. Laurent. Mr. St Laurent had been handling family issues for over ten years. He was the savviest attorney in his field, despite his grubby appearance and thinning grey hair. His suit, while not off the rack, looked slept in, and his nose was rosy and splotched. Tonya grimaced as he slurped his coffee before setting it on the table.

"Okay, tomorrow is the big day. Tiffany, because of your age, your role is pivotal," said St. Laurent.

"All of this mess is childish. Why can't I just say that I want to live with my mother, and we all get on with our lives? This is so embarrassing."

St. Laurent's assistant scribbled on his legal pad, "Good, say that in court, let's keep practicing."

"For what, I'm tired of this."

Tonya placed her hand over Trixie's, "Baby, please, I know this is hard, but I haven't been the best parent, and his lawyer will capitalize on that. I need you to do this for us," said Tonya.

"Tiffany, describe the relationship you have with your mother," said St. Laurent.

"Do you have to call me, Tiffany?"

"Yep, so get used to it. It fits the image we are trying to portray."

"Well, life with my mother is okay." Mr. St. Laurent's assistant scribbled on a notepad.

"It's wonderful," interrupted St. Laurent.

"It's wonderful; we shop. We take vacations to Europe, and I eat at the finest restaurants. It's any teenager's dream life."

"All wrong, you sound like you're talking about your nanny, not your mother," said St. Laurent.

"Well, it's the truth," said Trixie. St. Laurent leaned back in his chair and stared at an imaginary spot on the wall.

"Try this. Life with my mom is wonderful. We do a lot of things together. It's just us, but I like it that way. It made us have a close relationship, almost like friends, but she still lays down the law."

St Laurent's assistant took over the questioning, "Tell me about some of the things you and your mother do together."

St. Laurent cleared his throat, "Really cool stuff. We take trips to Europe, we do girly stuff like makeovers and shopping, and sometimes we eat at the best restaurants. She says that one day I'm going to have to know how to carry myself among high society. That's what I love about my mother. She believes in me," finished St Laurent with a satisfied grin.

"You expect me to remember all that?

Tonya squeezed Trixie's hand, "Just try please. I know there has to be something you love about me," said Tonya.

"It has to sound genuine. I'm not telling you to lie, but you need to rearrange the worst of the past. Lawrence's lawyer is good, and he is going to pull out all the guns," said St. Laurent.

"Plus, we went to school together, so he knows a lot," added Tonya.

Trixie took a deep breath and tried again, "I love my momma. We don't have the perfect relationship, but I wouldn't trade what we have for anyone, including my father."

Trixie brushed her hair out of her eye and glanced at her mother. Tonya nodded.

"It would be cool getting to know him, but I'm a young woman now, and I'm just getting to know myself. I need my mom to guide me and push me to pursue my wildest dreams. I know my dad is hurting, but all of this bickering and his unwillingness to take my wishes into account is pushing me away from him."

Trixie paused and took a deep breath, "Please don't tear our family apart. I want my father in my life, so he can school me on boys and everything, but I want to live with my mother. I think I can grow to love him, but that's just the way it is."

"That's right on the money," said. St Laurent.

"Did you mean all that," asked Tonya.

"Yea." Tonya leaned over and embraced Trixie.

"Perfect, do that when she leaves the stand, and I'll have tissue ready for you two. Now Tonya, let's discuss your job as a financial planner and work on Lawrence's background information," said St. Laurent.

"I have a graduate degree in Finance, and I work from

home advising and managing portfolios for a few select clients. I recently used my contacts and previous experience to land a job writing articles for several business and lifestyle magazines. In fact, my PR person is working on scheduling me as a guest on various news programs and talk shows."

"You have an agent, mom? Why do you need those different men?"

"Listen, Trixie, I've done more than I should have."

Mr. St. Laurent placed his coffee on the table, "Not today you haven't or next week or the week after. I hate to interrupt this mother-daughter moment, but as far as I am concerned, any man your mother has interacted with were business colleagues and mentors. The courts understand the struggle of single mothers," said St. Laurent as his assistant passed him a handkerchief for his forehead.

Tonya ignored Mr. St. Laurent, "Baby, most of my business associates are for leverage and stability. Relationships are important in life. Remember that."

"Tiffany, let me and your mother finish up here. We have a lot of ground to cover, and you'd just get bored," said St. Laurent.

Trixie left the room and for the next few hours St. Laurent grilled Tonya on her childhood, her relationship with her parents, and everything she knew about Lawrence from the moment they met. She answered questions about every man she kept as friends. St. Laurent and his assistant were relentless. They twisted and manipulated information to make Lawrence look like the stereotypical man who abandoned his family. At the end of the session, Tonya was positive she had done right to keep a few secrets about Trixie's past. She would hate to have her attorney expose Trixie's past behavior unnecessarily.

EPISODE EIGHT

DIRTY LAUNDRY

Awana stared at the empty shelves and wiped at the pool of sweat that trickled down her blouse. Mingled with the stench of hard work, were the tears she struggled to keep at bay all morning. In the distance, she could hear Lawrence's favorite show blaring from the flat-screen television she purchased for his birthday.

"Lawrence, are you going to carry my bags to the car?" said Awana as she prepared to leave behind her marriage and its memories. Frustrated that Lawrence ignored her, she dragged her suitcases to the door. She paused to grab some last-minute items from the hall closet, when she noticed a large manila folder hidden beneath a stack of papers. Curious, she opened the folder and rifled through pictures of Judge Mendleson and a teenage girl. There was also a report from a private investigation firm.

"Lawrence, what is all of this? Why do you have pictures of Judge Mendleson and his daughter?" asked Awana as she barged into the family room. Lawrence snatched the folder out of Awana's hands and slung it on the sofa.

"Haven't you done enough without going through my personal business?"

"I know you are not tripping over papers I found in our closet. This doesn't even compare to you snooping through my office."

Lawrence tossed the folder on the sofa, "Whatever, just leave. None of this is your concern anymore."

"It is my concern if it concerns Trixie. You could get in serious trouble with this information in your possession."

"Don't pretend to be concerned with my welfare or my daughter's. If you were concerned, you'd be helping make sure I get custody. I knew I couldn't trust you. That's why I handled things myself."

"Court hasn't started. Things may go your way," said Awana.

Lawrence turned and looked at his future ex-wife, "Since when has the court worked in the best interest of a black man?"

"It will work. You're not some gang banging drug pusher."

"Listen at you, getting all high and mighty on me. We should have never married."

"We married because we love each other. We wanted to represent black love the right way."

"Save it. You married me because I made your coochie sing."

Awana slapped Lawrence's face, then slapped him again.

Lawrence jerked away from Awana, rubbing his face, "Leave my house."

"I have no choice but to see Judge Mendleson. I wish you would reconsider." Awana picked up her purse and turned to leave.

"Wait."

"I'm sorry things are hard, but I should have never

placed my hands on you. I can't believe we have come to this. I don't like myself right now," said Awana.

"Please sit down. Let me explain."

"There is nothing left to discuss."

"A few years ago, his stepdaughter ran away and joined an extremist group in West Texas. When they convinced her to come home, he and his wife spent thousands of dollars on rehab and psychiatric counseling, but she kept having issues.

Awana took a seat on the sofa. Lawrence sat next to her, wanting to brush her hair behind her ear the way she did when she was nervous, but he didn't have that right anymore. He scooted away from her.

"Eventually, her biological father got sole custody after he claimed they were unfit parents. If Mendleson rules in Tonya's favor, I plan to appeal based on his inability to be impartial."

"It sounds like a long shot that could really damage your chances with Trixie. Is it worth going through all of this? Since you found out Trixie was your daughter, you've changed. You lose your temper at the slightest provocation, and your inability to forgive has destroyed our marriage. What's next?" asked Awana.

"I wouldn't expect you to understand."

"Why, because I don't have any children? Doesn't that make me the only rational one here? I'm afraid you may gain custody of your child but lose your daughter."

"That's a chance I have to take. I still love you and when this is over Trixie is going to need you, and so will I. Stay with me and help me fight Tonya." Lawrence grasped Awana's hands and silently willed her to come back to him.

"I can't. If I thought this was more about Trixie than revenge on Tonya I would. I think your feelings are hurt, so you are determined to make Tonya pay. Don't you see that's the wrong motive? Baby, please forget the case and let's work together on building our family, you, me and Trixie."

Lawrence dropped his head and walked into the bedroom. Awana stood a moment longer then gathered the evidence that could determine the fate of so many lives.

EPISODE NINE

DIRTY DRAWS

Tonya scuttled behind security trying not to bump into anyone as they escorted her into the courthouse.

"I just don't understand why the media is here," said Tonya as security shuffled them into the courthouse.

"Anytime St. Laurent is handling a case, it's big news," said St. Laurent's assistant.

"At least he looks camera ready. I was worried he'd come looking like a homeless person," said Tonya.

Once both parties settled in the courtroom, the judge addressed everyone.

"Let me start by saying I was disappointed to get the final notice that both parents failed to agree regarding the custody of Tiffany Peterson. I want each argument presented succinctly. I will not tolerate the antics both attorneys are capable of, and if any party gets out of line I will clear this courtroom. Mr. Evans, you may begin."

"Your honor, for the past fifteen years, my client's natural right to be a father was denied. Fifteen years ago, my client pleaded with the mother of Tonya Peterson for the opportunity to speak with her daughter. He wanted her to know he loved her and his unborn child; he wanted to marry Tonya, but had the door slammed in his face.

At the rear of the courtroom, Tonya's mother sat with her head high, comforted by Grant. Max took a few steps forward, making sure the pin on his lapel was prominent. It was a subtle reminder to the judge they were a part of the same law fraternity. Lawrence and the boys roasted him because he chose to pledge a white professional fraternity, but over the years, much of his success came from those connections.

"Mrs. Peterson thought she was protecting her daughter. What mother wouldn't? But it was Tonya Peterson who sealed the deal. For fifteen years, she lived in the same city as my client, yet not one time did she attempt to contact him. Hell, she could have at least put him on child support.

Judge Mendleson banged the gavel on his desk, "Mr. Evans."

"Sorry, but my client has less than three years to get to know the child he has loved sight unseen. He should be allowed to spend the maximum time with his daughter."

"Mr. Evans, your client was done a disservice, but his daughter is old enough to decide her living arrangements. Is there any plausible reason I should not concur with Tiffany's desire to stay with her mother and award Mr. Thompson visitation?" asked Judge Mendleson.

"My client is concerned with his daughter's moral upbringing. Tonya Peterson's income is sketchy, yet she lives in a luxury home and drives a luxury vehicle."

"Since when is it a crime to live well counselor? Do you have anything else?

Before he and his wife spent sizeable sums of money on his stepdaughter's recovery, Judge Mendleson enjoyed spending his money on exclusive memberships and real estate. His goal was to have several properties on each continent to visit on vacations and then eventually retire. Most of the homes he owned he sold or leased for additional income to cover his daughter's rehab. The only home he kept was his primary residence and a small place in Greece he gifted his wife on their tenth anniversary.

"My client believes that Tonya Peterson is into high priced prostitution."

Lawrence dropped his head. He hated Trixie had to hear this.

"Mr. Evans, I've reviewed the documentation provided to this court regarding both parties' finances. Managing portfolios and writing scholarly articles hardly qualify as sex work."

"All I meant was that a woman of questionable reputation is not the best influence for an impressionable teenager."

"Your honor, I object. Tiffany is an honor student at a magnet school and a part of the youth group at church," said St. Laurent.

"Mr. St. Laurent, you will have your moment. Mr. Evans you are trying my patience. I will not make a ruling based on morality preferences. If you have proof that Tiffany in is in danger living with her mother spit it out. Otherwise, stop wasting this court's time." said Judge Mendleson.

"Sorry, Sir."

Max took a moment and then continued, "Yes, Trixie is an honor student, but she is also in counseling for anger management and promiscuity issues your honor."

"And how do you know this?" asked Mr. Mendleson.

"Mrs. Thompson, my client's wife, was Tiffany's therapist."

"This sounds like privileged information."

Lawrence turned to look at Awana and then stood from behind the table. "Sir, I would like to answer that question for myself."

"Very well, you may approach. I've got a feeling this will be a long morning."

Lawrence sat on the witness stand and looked at his family. His parents and his older brother came to show their support, and he needed their strength because after his testimony, he was not positive he wouldn't lose his wife and his daughter.

"Mr. Thompson, can you start from the beginning," asked Max.

"A brief synopsis please," said Judge Mendleson.

"When Tonya and I met, we were both seniors, and my football career had just ended the year before, so my future was murky. Tonya, however, had dozens of offers from financial firms across the country. When she told me she was pregnant I panicked. I felt like half a man supported by his woman."

"So, you went away to get your thoughts together?" asked Max.

"I know I should have called, but I knew if I heard Tonya's voice, I would have responded off emotion."

"When you returned, what happened?"

Tonya turned to look at her parents. She only knew fragments of what happened next, so she was eager to hear the entire truth.

"I went straight to Tonya's house." Lawrence paused and took a deep breath in a moment of indecision.

"Well, when I got there, Mrs. Peterson answered the door. She looked like a mad woman. She was waving the Bible in my face and yelling, 'There are no sinners in my house.'"

Judge Mendleson shifted in his seat, "Mr. Thompson, could you describe what you meant when you said Mrs. Peterson looked like a mad woman?"

Mr. St. Laurent stood and cleared his throat,

"Respectfully your honor, Mrs. Peterson's demeanor has no bearing on the outcome of that meeting. Mr. Thompson had years to build a relationship with his daughter, but he didn't. Instead, he built a life with another woman. Now, I believe he was faithful and didn't have side children like his father, but he still ignored his firstborn."

"Are you kidding me," yelled one of Lawrence's brothers. During the chaos, Valerie mouthed, "Tonya, stop this."

Tonya pretended not to see Valerie. *"That's cold-blooded,"* she thought as Judge Mendleson banged his gavel. Max motioned for Lawrence to remain calm.

"Bailiff, if anyone other than those I have invited to speak opens his mouth. Take them to jail."

"Mr. Thompson, what happened next?" questioned Max.

"I left. I sat in my car and thought about calling the police."

Tonya exhaled and smacked her lips. Her lawyer applied pressure to her forearm.

"May I add something?" Max looked at Lawrence. They hadn't rehearsed Lawrence going rogue.

"Tonya told me a while back that her mother was a religious fanatic. Sometimes she would sleep in the church. Her husband left her because of her crazy ideas."

Tonya grabbed the notepad on the table to explain Lawrence's lies to Mr. St. Laurent. Lawrence stared at Awana. He hoped she understood he was trying not to use the information he had against the judge.

"Your honor, Mrs. Peterson came to the door with a rag on her head wearing a long white dress. Once Tonya showed me an altar room where her mother had candles burning. It looked like some bizarre ritual. The night I came to see Tonya, I was frantic. I didn't know if she had killed Tonya and my baby. She was always talking about demons and stuff."

"Now that's bizarre," said Max. What do you know about Tonya's life now?"

"Let's wait on that piece of information until after a fifteen-minute break," interrupted Judge Mendleson.

Max ushered Lawrence to the side of the courtroom.

"What the hell are you doing?"

"Winning my case," said Lawrence walking towards his parents.

Lawrence's family looked like the typical black family dressed in their go to church attire. The men wore button-down shirts with slacks and a matching tie. His mother had on an A-line dress and a pair of navy shoes with a block heel. Her twists were in a neat bun.

"How long is this going to take," asked Lawrence's younger brother.

"Why you got warrants?" asked the older brother.

Lawrence's mother sat nervously, fiddling with a hand-kerchief, "Are you sure court is the right move?"

"He's fighting for my granddaughter," said Lawrence's father. "I'm going to introduce myself to Tiffany."

"Aren't you afraid you'll do irreparable harm? Tiffany may not want to deal with you again," said Lawrence's mother.

"I know what I'm doing, mother." Minutes later, Judge Mendleson came back into the courtroom, and Max continued questioning Lawrence.

"Mr. Peterson, can you tell me about your daughter's living situation based on what you have seen since you've been in her life?"

"Well, my first experience with Tiffany was when I heard rumors about the new girl at the youth center."

"New girl being Tiffany?" asked Max pointing at Trixie.

"Yeah, some boys said they heard that if you get on her good side, she'd hook you up," said Lawrence.

"With sex?"

"I'm not sure, which is one reason I'm desperate to provide her with guidance. I don't want her to be like her mother."

"Before the break you mentioned Trixie was sent to counseling for some disturbing things. How do you know this?"

Lawrence shifted in his seat, "I took my wife's file cabinet keys and read Tiffany's case file. I know it was wrong, but I was desperate after I learned what happened between Tiffany and her school counselor. I had to see what kind of life Tonya was exposing my child to."

"Mr. Evans," said Judge Mendleson. "Let me stop you. I want to control the information regarding the minor Tiffany Peterson in open court. Mrs. Thompson, will you please take the stand? Mr. Thompson, have a seat."

"But," protested Lawrence.

"That will be all Mr. Thompson," said Judge Mendleson.

Lawrence and Awana passed each other on the way to their respective seats. Awana glared at Lawrence, trying to catch his attention, but he wouldn't look her way.

"Mrs. Thompson, in the interest of the minor Tiffany Peterson, I need you to disclose all the information you obtained in your sessions that may be pertinent to the suitability of Tonya Peterson as a parent," said Judge Mendleson.

"I'm sorry, but I can't do that."

"Are you aware that I can get a court order for this information?"

"And I still won't disclose the information. My job is to protect Trixie. There is nothing I can tell you that will further this case."

"I am the only one that can determine that. This court will take a two-hour break while I obtain the documentation to force Mrs. Thompson's testimony. Please be advised Mrs. Thompson that you will speak, or I will have you placed in custody."

When the judge left the courtroom, the only people remaining were the attorneys and their teams. Tonya knew Lawrence and his attorney would pursue this line of questioning, so she was prepared.

"Trixie, I am so sorry you have to go through this. If only Lawrence would settle out of court," said Tonya.

"I know mom, but let's not discuss it. It's not as if everything he is saying is untrue."

"The distorted truth," said Tonya's father.

"Tonya, have lunch with me. We need to talk."

"I don't feel like getting into anything heavy," said Tonya.

"This is important. There are some things about your mother you need to know."

"It's her and her crazy ideas that could make me lose this case."

"You can't blame grandma for that mom. You haven't spoken to her in years. You did this when you refused to let my dad in my life," said Trixie.

"Tonya please," said her father.

Lawrence's parents made their way to Tonya and Trixie. Unlike her hardheaded son, she understood they needed a truce between the two families.

"Tonya, I hate that after so many years, we have to see each other in a courtroom."

"Blame that on your son," said Tonya.

"Listen, I don't agree with what he's doing. I think you two should share custody. But you know my son, can't tell him anything."

"Yeah, but this is a new low even for him," said Tonya turning her back.

"My husband and I would like you and Tiffany to share lunch with us. Lawrence won't be coming."

"Dream on," said Trixie. "Not after how you people are treating my mother," said Trixie.

Eventually, everyone split up for lunch. Trixie went with her grandmother while Tonya and her father left together.

Tonya and her father settled into the booth of a restaurant down from the courthouse. Tonya ordered a tuna sandwich on rye with a glass of green tea, while her father had a wing special with an extra helping of fries.

"Dad, you're too old to be eating like that. Have you had your cholesterol checked lately?"

"I'm as healthy as a mule."

"And as stubborn," said Tonya.

"Well, you inherited that."

"Don't forget, Trixie. Once that girl sets her mind on something, there's no stopping her," laughed Tonya.

"She's such a beautiful girl. I wished I could have watched her grow. I should have camped out at your house, your job, anything to get back in your life. Letting you push me away was the biggest mistake of my life."

Tonya reached across the table and snagged one of her father's fries. "I'm so sorry. I just couldn't accept the fact that my mother discarded me after I got pregnant."

"I take a lot of the blame for that. I was good at running away. I'd retreat in my corner and let your mother have the run of things. I should have been more of a man."

"But daddy, you were great. I shouldn't have kept you out of my life because of my anger at mom. At first, I took the divorce personally. Like you were divorcing me. After a while, one year turned into two, then five, six. By that time, I had too much pride to say I was wrong."

Grant stirred the ice in his drink, "I knew what your mother's religious ideals were doing to the family; I was just too much of a coward to do anything about it.

Grant grabbed both of Tonya's hands, "You have to understand what your mother did was out of misguided love."

"It hurt that she wasn't in the delivery room."

"I know, baby, but she wanted to be. Her mind was screwed up. You know your mother is not in a cult, right?"

"Yes, I know."

"So, what made you go back to her?" asked Tonya.

"Love?"

"Come on, you can do better than that."

"She came back to me. If you want any other details, you got to talk to her."

"Thank you for supporting me, daddy. I may not be the best mother, but I love my baby. It'll kill me to lose her."

Grant came around the table and hugged Tonya, "Me too, sweetie. It'll kill me too."

The attorneys ushered their clients into the judge's chambers. Judge Mendleson provided the paperwork needed to compel Awana's testimony, but she felt more comfortable in closed quarters. Trixie stayed in the courtroom, along with both sides of her family.

"Mrs. Thompson, do you understand that you are still under oath?"

"Yes, your honor," said Awana as Judge Mendleson began his questioning.

"Please describe the circumstances that brought Tiffany to counseling," said the judge.

"Ms. Peterson and her school principal agreed that Trixie needed counseling for her troubling behavior," said Awana.

"Please be more specific."

"Trixie was caught performing oral sex on several classmates. Although it can't be verified, we believe this was an ongoing issue. I received Trixie as a client after an incident with the school's counselor.

"When Tiffany came to counseling, did she confirm she was engaging in this behavior?" questioned Judge Mendleson.

"Eventually."

"What about the relationship with her mother?"

"The first few sessions, she expressed concern that her mother only loved her if she made good grades and played a certain role. They weren't very close."

"What did she say about her mother's character?"

"Dubious."

"In your professional opinion, do you believe that Tiffany needs to be placed with her father?"

Afraid of what Awana would say, Lawrence elbowed his attorney.

"Your honor, this witness is prejudiced. She should not be asked to make a decision that involves her husband," said Max.

"I'm afraid she has too. She is a licensed professional, and I trust her to remain professional."

Awana looked at her husband. She knew her answer would seal the fate of their marriage.

"I believe Trixie would benefit from knowing both of her parents equally. I recommend Tonya and Trixie attend family counseling. I see no reason she shouldn't maintain at least partial custody," said Awana.

"Thank you, Mrs. Thompson, everyone let's return to the courtroom."

"May I have a moment to myself," said Awana.

"Of course, you can wait outside. My assistant will lead you into the courtroom when you're ready," said Judge Mendleson.

Back in the courtroom, Tonya scanned the room from the witness stand. She smiled briefly at Pastor Donnelly. Her parents huddled together in the corner while Lawrence's family appeared confident. For the first time, Tonya looked at Trixie and saw an impressionable girl. When Trixie entered high school, she assumed she didn't have to provide as much parental guidance as she did when she was younger. Now she realized that while Trixie didn't need a babysitter or to have her face and fingers cleaned, she still needed a firm but loving hand. She failed.

Hopefully, I can get this straight, thought Tonya as she waited for her lawyer to begin.

"Ms. Peterson, you've heard Mr. Thompson say some harsh things here today."

"Most of what he said was barely the truth. I understand he is resentful, but he went too far. I offered to share custody with him, but he refused. All of this is a vendetta against me. Otherwise, he would have never subjected our daughter to this kind of ridicule."

"Tell me what happened the night Lawrence visited your mother."

"I never knew he came. I had a big argument with my mother because I stood by Lawrence even though it had been two weeks since we last spoke."

"After you had Tiffany, why didn't you try to contact Lawrence?"

"Hurt, foolish, angry, prideful, I wanted to prove to everyone that I didn't need a man to raise a well-rounded daughter."

"Can you please explain to everyone why you call your daughter Trixie?"

"It was a rebellious move against my mother. My mother would call the fast girls in my neighborhood tricks. I knew she wanted all the females in our family to have names that began with a "T," so I lied and told her that Trixie was Tiffany's birth name. It stuck after that."

"What about your mother's religious ideals?"

"She believes Jesus Christ is the son of God. She believes in the Holy Trinity. She is not and never has been in a cult."

"But what about the attire he saw her in that night?"

"She had just gotten back from communion service. The rag on her head was probably a scarf."

"And the candles, the altar?" asked St. Laurent.

"I don't see the problem. Catholics say Novenas and light candles."

"Ms. Peterson, are you willing to share custody with Tiffany's father?"

"Not anymore." Lawrence shifted in his seat and whispered in his lawyer's ear.

"Please explain."

"I'm afraid of what he may do to her." Lawrence's father jumped to his feet in outrage.

"You can't blacken my son's character."

"Sir, sit down, or you will be escorted out and banned from the rest of these proceedings," said Judge Mendleson.

Mr. Thompson threw a disgusted look at Tonya before leaving the courtroom with his wife following him.

"Ms. Peterson are you exaggerating to make Mr. Thompson look unfit?" continued St. Laurent.

"No, I forgot about his violent temper until he came to speak with me one night,"

"What happened that night?"

"See for yourself, I recorded it with my nanny cam."

Tonya's statement caused a major ruckus in the court-room, and the judge threatened to close the proceedings.

"Your honor, this is ridiculous. You said you didn't want theatrics, yet Mr. St. Laurent and his client are turning this into a circus," objected Max.

"I agree, please explain Mr. St. Laurent."

"Ms. Peterson is a concerned parent who only wants to show the court why Mr. Thompson should not be awarded custody of his daughter. We are, however, amendable to supervised visitation."

"Do not insult my intelligence by even suggesting supervised visitation for a fifteen-year-old," said Judge Mendleson.

"Judge, please allow me a little leniency. I believe the video will prove insightful."

"I'll allow it."

Tonya's attorney connected the camera to the court's television, and everyone witnessed Lawrence grabbing Tonya by the neck.

"Show the rest of the tape. She's trying to set me up," railed Lawrence.

"Mr. Evans control your client," boomed Judge Mendleson.

Awana attempted to walk towards the front of the room, "Judge, I swear on my license Tonya was never in any trouble. This video looks worse than it is. Tonya and I have had several friendly conversations after this event and even went to lunch."

"I have never put my hands on a woman. Tonya! Why would you do this in front of our child?"

The security guard grabbed Lawrence by the arm and pushed him in his seat.

"I'm warning you one last time," said Judge Mendleson.

Mr. St. Laurent shifted towards the prosecutor's table so only Lawrence and his attorney could see his satisfied grin.

"Ms. Peterson, were there any other instances where Lawrence lost his temper?"

"Well, they suspended him from the football team a few times for unnecessary roughness and fighting teammates."

Lawrence squeezed his fists together, rocking back and forth. St. Laurent took a deep exaggerated breath.

"Ms. Peterson, what is your relationship like with Tiffany now?"

"Great, our adversity strengthened us. I'm in counseling and taking parenting classes. I started several months ago because I wanted to be a better mother. It's as if Tiffany and I are just meeting each other for the first time."

After Tonya's stellar display, the judge dismissed court for the day. Back at Tonya's house, everything was quiet. Tonya stared at a cooking show on TV and Trixie went to her room to call Vince.

"It's been mad crazy. My mom's been exaggerating how bad a person my dad is, and my dad's been sticking it to my mother all the way around."

"Man, that sounds like it should be on a talk show," said Vince.

"Yep, and I'm the guest of honor tomorrow."

Vince walked into his closet and looked through some clothes balled up in a laundry basket. He pulled out a white polo shirt, shaking it to release the wrinkles.

"Would you like me to come?" asked Vince.

"I'm not sure. Things have been personal."

"It's all good, you know a brother got your back," said Vince.

"Yeah, I know. I'll just be glad when all of this crap is over."

"So, do you think your dad and Awana will get back together?"

"I hope so; he's being such an idiot. Right now, I feel neutral with the whole custody thing." Trixie pulled off her shirt and slacks and lay on her back under the ceiling fan.

"But didn't you say your dad did some screwed up things in court today?"

"Yea. I'm flattered that he is fighting hard for me, but he is bashing my momma."

"My mom and I can barely be in the same room without going at it, but nobody better step to her."

"Are things better between you and her?"

"She's been to the apartment twice and cooked a few meals."

"You may as well come to court tomorrow; I'll probably need the support." said Trixie hanging up the phone.

J udge Mendleson's court convened at 9:00 a.m. Only Tonya and Lawrence's parents, Pastor Donnelly, and Vince were present. In the far corner was a single reporter from a local newspaper. Judge Mendleson entered the courtroom with a thick manila folder and shared a few whispered words with his assistant.

"Tiffany Peterson, will you please take the stand?" Trixie approached the witness stand dressed in a pair of expensive slacks and a pale pink blouse with a bow on the front. Her hair flowed in loose curls, and her jewelry was minimal. She looked like a flourishing teenager. Once Trixie sat, the judge gave the order of the day's proceedings.

"The last person to testify will be Tiffany. I will handle the questioning. Once I have finished, I will sift through everything I have heard the last two days and then make my decision. Does everyone understand?

Judge Mendleson turned to Trixie and gave her a friendly smile, "Tiffany, tell me about life with your mother?"

"It's cool, we have a good relationship. My mother and I like the same things, and we spend a lot of time together."

"Has it always been that way?"

"Pretty much."

Judge Mendleson consulted the manila folder, "It says here you expressed concern to your counselor that your mother only cared if you projected the appearance of being a well-rounded teen. What did you mean about that?"

Trixie looked confidently at the judge, "Awana helped me to understand my reasoning was off. When I went to counseling, I believed because my mother pushed so hard school was all she cared about. Now I see it was parental pride and love. It made me want to work harder."

For added effect, Trixie beamed an all-American smile at her mother. Mr. St. Laurent cheered inwardly.

"What specific incident caused your mother to seek counseling for you?" asked the judge continuing his questioning.

"A misunderstanding with a classmate."

"This will go easier if, from this point, you answer honestly and completely. This court has your best interest as its key concern. You can be an enormous help by telling me what I need to know," said Judge Mendleson.

"A girl blasted me in front of the entire class about my personal business."

"Was it your mother's idea or the principal's idea for you to attend counseling?"

"I don't know."

"Tiffany, what was your mother's response to all the trouble you got into at school?"

"She said I needed to stop the behavior."

"And?"

"That's all."

Judge Mendleson gave Tiffany a nod of encouragement, "Do you blame your mother for how your life turned out?"

Trixie looked at her mother. She knew the courtroom

was not the place to express her feelings, but it all poured out.

"I think she had an idea of what I was doing, but never said a word. I could have had help a long time ago."

At the back of the courtroom, Vince shook his head no, and Pastor Donnelly shifted in his seat.

"Tiffany, tell me about your mother's male companions."

"You mean her sugar daddies." Trixie heard her mother's swift intake of breath and realized too late that her joke fell flat.

"I'm sorry, bad joke," said Trixie, but no one in the courtroom believed Trixie's poor attempt at trying to cover her hasty speech.

"Tiffany, how does your mother earn a living?"

"She's a financial adviser."

"Do you know what that means?" asked Judge Mendleson. St. Laurent's assistant stood, "Your honor, I must object. The complexities involved in financial planning make it unlikely my client would discuss her work with her daughter."

Judge Mendleson looked at St. Laurent's assistant with a raised eyebrow. Max allowed himself a brief smirk while St. Laurent passed his assistant a reprimand on a folded slip of paper.

"Tiffany, your response?" asked Judge Mendleson.

"I'm not into her work."

"What about overnight guests?"

"Never."

"Does she accept money or gifts from her lovers?" asked Judge Mendleson.

"Who doesn't?"

Judge Mendleson covered his smirk with a fake cough, "Tiffany, the paperwork provided by your father's attorney stated that your mother has men in and out of your home. Is that true?"

"Not really."

"Are you aware of any gifts she has received?"

"Objection, my client is an attractive woman. Receiving gifts from an admirer hardly makes her a prostitute," said St. Laurent.

"Overruled. Tiffany, to your knowledge, were these items paid for by one person or several?"

Trixie glanced at her mother then dropped her head, "Several."

"What types of items were your mother gifted?"

Trixie remained silent until Tonya nodded her head. "Her SUV, house bill, jewelry, trips." Judge Mendleson took a moment to jot a few notes in his folder.

"I know your mother has been working on her personal issues. Is it because she set her sights on a minister?"

Trixie looked at her Lawrence and rolled her eyes.

"Why does any of that matter? You wouldn't know that information if my dad hadn't stolen my confidential files."

"Tiffany, do you want to live with your father?"

"No, I want to get to know him, but I want to stay with my mother."

"Okay, one last question. When did you first tell your mother about the inappropriate behavior of your school counselor, Mr. Clayton?"

At the mention of Trixie's school counselor, the reporter in the corner snapped to attention.

"Uhhh, two days later, maybe."

"How did she respond?" asked Judge Mendleson.

St. Laurent gave Tonya a hard look. He was aware of the situation between Trixie and her former counselor, but he dreaded Trixie's answer. His senses were at full alert, and they were signifying disaster. Tonya sat stone-faced while

Trixie waited for the signal to walk out of the courtroom and leave the judge to find his own answers.

"At first, she thought, I tried to bargain my way out of the session."

"And then?"

"She told me if someone was messing with me, bite it off and save a piece for her."

"How soon after this conversation was Mr. Clayton's behavior reported to the principal and the police?"

"I don't know."

"Did anyone at school ever follow up with you regarding this issue?"

"No."

"Did she ever speak with you again about what occurred with Mr. Clayton?"

"No."

Judge Mendleson took a deep breath, "Tiffany, how did you meet your current counselor, Mrs. Thompson?"

"She saw me walking home from school and gave me a ride."

By this time, Lawrence had a huge grin on his face, and Max was struggling to keep him calm.

"Did your mother interview other counselors after you stopped seeing Mr. Clayton?"

"No, Pastor Donnelly recommended Awana. My mother makes sure she receives quality services."

"Last question, I promise." Before the judge could begin, Tonya stood and banged her fist on the table.

"Enough," said Tonya as she pushed St. Laurent's hand off her shoulder.

"My daughter will not suffer a moment longer for my transgressions. Pastor Donnelly volunteered to speak with Trixie, but I shot the idea down. I did not want the man I intended to know on a personal level privy to the sordid details of my family life. Yes, I screwed up. I should have responded to Trixie's concerns about Mr. Clayton in a timelier manner. Now make your decision and leave my daughter alone."

Judge Mendleson gathered his papers and stood, "Ms. Peterson is correct. I have all the information I need. Tiffany, thank you. You did well. Everyone go home and rest. I doubt I will have a ruling today."

EPISODE ELEVEN

LANE CHANGE

The mood at the Peterson's house was somber.

Trixie and Tonya walked on eggshells around one another, each afraid to free the torrent of emotions they held in check. Trixie shut up in her room, trying to ignore her hunger pains. Tonya chose to make herself available if Trixie wanted to talk by watching television in the living room but refused to give in completely and seek Trixie first. Pastor Donnelly's arrival was a welcome distraction from Tonya's gloomy thoughts, and it allowed Trixie a chance to sprint into the kitchen for a sandwich.

"Pastor Donnelly, what are you doing here?" asked Tonya opening the door.

"I just wanted to spread a little cheer. I hope you like wildflowers."

"Thank you so much, I didn't think you would want to see me again after the courtroom drama today."

Tonya walked into the living room ahead of Pastor Donnelly. She believed he was probably planning to break off their association and ask her to find another church. She would miss her church. After the turmoil of the past few months, she realized how much she needed a strong Christian foundation to continue the progress she made towards changing her life.

"I'm glad you're here."

"Did you think I would stay away?" asked Pastor Donnelly, shrugging out of his coat.

"Well, I wasn't sure what to expect. I've pushed you away and been disrespectful when you've only been supportive."

"Tonya, I've told you before no one is perfect. We have a long way to go before our friendship develops into anything deeper if it ever does. But to pretend you are just another church member is not acceptable. I want to see where this will lead, but I must also consider my role as pastor. The woman I associate myself with will play a pivotal role in helping to maintain my church and support my purpose."

"Wow, I wasn't expecting all that. You must have been a smooth talker back in the day."

"I'm not saying a word, it may incriminate me later. So, how's Trixie holding up?" asked Pastor Donnelly, shrugging out of his jacket.

"I haven't heard a word from her since we got home from court."

"She's young, and this has been a lot for her to handle. I'm sure things will get back to normal soon."

"Well, I hope everything won't return to normal. My kind of normal is not acceptable to me anymore. I really am trying to change."

"Yes, you are, and I will be there all the way," said Pastor Donnelly giving Tonya a hug.

"Thank you, I really need the support but only as a friend.

"I didn't come here to pressure you, just to offer my support and see if you've spoken to Trixie about what the future will look like if the outcome isn't in your favor?"

"No, I'm trying to stay positive. Where are you going with all of this?" asked Tonya.

"I think you need her to be prepared as a precaution. She may be dealing with anxiety."

"If she is anxious, it's her fault. You were there. You saw how she almost betrayed me before I interrupted."

"Betrayed you!" Trixie slammed her cup of juice on the kitchen table and stormed into the living room.

"I'm the one who should be upset right now. You betrayed me all my life by refusing to be a mother and keeping me from my father."

"I have apologized for that more than once, and I will not let you keep holding my shortcomings over my head. You should have stuck to the plan and kept your mouth shut as we practiced. You made me appear unfit," shouted Tonya in Trixie's face.

"No one can make up anything without the proper ingredients. You're just mad I told the truth. Maybe I needed to get that off my chest after all these years. I'm sick of you seeking sympathy from everyone."

"I will not have you talking to me like this. Go to your room."

"Fine, but I hope you enjoy bossing me around because you won't get the chance once Lawrence comes to get me."

"What's that supposed to mean? Trixie, you come back here and answer me right now!"

"Tonya, she didn't mean what she said. She's just angry and stressed. It'll blow over," said Pastor Donnelly.

Tonya plopped down on the sofa folding her knees to her chest. Pastor Donnelly sat next to her placing his arm on her shoulder. Tonya turned her face to the wall.

"You should leave," said Tonya.

"But-."

"You want to be my friend? Then leave like I'm asking

you. A friendship is all I have to give and that will probably go to hell."

Pastor Donnelly stood and walked towards the front door, "Tonya I'm not rushing anything. You're not the same person who invited me to dinner. I think we can have something good if we take our time."

"I don't need the additional complication."

***

Tonya closed the last of the boxes and sat on the floor staring at Trixie's empty space. Since there was only two weeks left in the school year, the judge allowed Lawrence to have Trixie until the beginning of August. After the blow-up, Trixie didn't want to come home and pack her things. It was as if she couldn't get away from her mother quick enough, but Tonya was not a quitter, and she was not about to adopt a new habit. Trixie would be back where she belonged, and she had thousands of dollars of surveillance equipment waiting to help seal the deal.

Trixie finished the last two weeks of school getting to know her father. It was so funny because she thought most of her habits and personality came from her mother, but she realized she was truly her father's kid. When they were together in public people would comment on how alike they looked. They found they both had a love for sports and video games. Trixie introduced Lawrence to her knowledge of fine foods, and Lawrence threw down on pig feet and neck bones, none of which she liked. Next month Lawrence was planning to take Trixie to Oklahoma to meet some of his extended family.

"When can I come and see you?" asked Vince.

"I don't know."

"How's your mom doing?"

"Don't want to talk about her. I haven't even spoken to her since the judge split me in two."

"Trixie don't go out like that. You should at least call and see how she is doing and even better, if you go for the weekend I can come and see you."

"I guess, but only because I miss you."

Tonya sat with her feet propped on the coffee table gnawing on Oreo cookies. The carpet had balls of lent and dishes were in the sink. Tonya didn't want it to seem like she prepared a Martha Stewart homecoming for Trixie. The only things that needed to be in place were the nanny cams and audio recorders. When Trixie called to say that she wanted to come for a visit, she prayed the opportunity had arrived for her to get enough dirt on Lawrence to bring her baby home. She had the entire house wired; all she had to do was wait for what came naturally.

"Chips and salsa are on the table in the kitchen," said Tonya as she passed Vince and Trixie in the hallway.

"Yeah, whatever."

"Girl you need to lighten up. You been dogging your momma since I got here. She's trying hard to be cool. She even let me chill in your room."

"You should have seen how jacked up the house was when I got here. I had to clean up so I wouldn't be embarrassed. I guess things have been hard on her with me staying at my dad's place."

"You need to stay in touch. Don't be acting all brand new since you met your dad. She may have been wrong for keeping him from you, but she still held it down. Hell, you were living the fab life."

"I guess I been tripping a bit. When I got here, I was bragging like living with my dad was so wonderful."

"It's cool, get your shine on, just don't dog your mom in the process."

"On the real, though, all the stuff my dad and I do could still be done if I were here with my mom. It's hard adjusting to living with a stranger, especially a man."

"Yo, he ain't try nothing with you, huh?"

"Nah, I don't think he like that. Although there was this one time, I forgot to lock the bathroom door, and he caught me getting out of the shower. I know it was a mistake, but it seemed like he stared a little too long."

"Dang, that's freaky getting caught by your dad like that. He got to see the goods before I did," said Vince dodging Trixie as she threw a bag of Doritos at his head.

"Seriously, though, what happened?"

"We barely spoke to each other for the next few days, and I started putting a chair under the doorknob in my room. It was just silly paranoia, but we finally had it out, and he said the only thing that was running through his mind was, did he have enough shotgun shells."

"Everybody dad says that same stuff. It didn't stop them when they were young and trying to smash."

"Fa real. After we talked, it was all good. I do miss my mom when I'm there."

"That's what's up. I'm really glad things are working out for you."

"Me too," said Trixie.

EPISODE TWELVE

WELL-GROOMED

C hris sat with his cell phone in his hand, scrolling through Trixie's social media account. He couldn't stop thinking about her. Missy reluctantly gave him Trixie's information when he threatened to tell her mother about the party she threw. She knew her mother was whipped and weak. He paid all the bills and ran his home like a man should. What he said was law, even if it divided mother and daughter. Missy knew what time it was. Trixie had been in his house, his bed. Everything and everyone in his house belonged to him. Chris logged out of his phone and let Trixie knock on the door a few more times. Finally, he put an angry look on his face and opened the door.

"Hi, Mr.-"

Chris walked off, leaving Trixie standing at the door.

"Is Missy here? Thank you for finding my earring. How did you get my number?" Trixie reluctantly entered the house as Chris walked down the hall without responding. Trixie stood nervously in the middle of the floor a few more moments when she heard Chris' voice raised in anger.

"I don't care if she is my mother. I don't owe her nothing."

Trixie turned to leave when Chris came back into the room.

"She put me up for adoption, and now she wants me to take care of her. For what? I don't even have children of my own, and it's hard being a stepfather because she jacked up my life. Man, let me call you back." Chris dropped the earring into Trixie's hand.

"This isn't mine. This looks like it came from Target," said Trixie.

"Well, I thought it was. Must be nice to have a mother who can afford expensive things."

Trixie took a step towards the door, "Sometimes."

Chris took a deep, loud breath, "When I was growing up, I prayed I would have a mother. I wasn't selfish. She didn't have to be mine. I just wanted someone to bake cookies and watch *Law and Order* with. It would be our show.

"My mom and I have a show, *227,*" said Trixie walking back into the room.

"I try to get Missy to watch TV with me. What's the one where the rapper takes her friends on a yacht?"

"I love that show. It's not ratchet-like other shows. I can see myself spending cash on my real friends like that."

Chris jumped up from his seat, "Want something to drink?"

"No, I gotta be going," said Trixie.

"You can't drink and drive?" asked Chris walking into the kitchen.

Trixie placed the earring on the table and waited by the door. Chris came back with a bottle of soda.

"Thanks for listening," he said handing Trixie the drink. He popped the tab, and the drink ran over her hands.

"Sorry about that. Wait right here for a paper towel."

Trixie stood by the door, wiping her hands on her shorts.

"Bottles up," said Chris handing Trixie the can and a paper towel.

"Come on, I'll walk you to your car." Chris walked Trixie to her BMW. He circled her car then convinced her the tires needed air. Trixie drove around the back of the house while Chris went to get his tire machine. He took his time checking the tire pressure and the car's fluid levels. Minutes later, Trixie was slumped over the steering wheel, barely conscious.

Awana pounded on Tonya's front door. Her hair was disheveled, and the sweatpants and t-shirt she wore had seen better days. Awana stepped back from the door as it opened. Tonya took a few steps outside, startled by Awana's appearance. *Splat.* Tonya reeled back as she felt a sting on her cheek. She pulled her arm back to charge Awana. It was obvious to Tonya that Awana had lived a privileged life, or she would have known once you swing, you don't stop until your opponent is on the ground, and a few hard kicks were delivered to the head. Thankfully, Tonya's brain was quicker than her fist because she remembered the video equipment attached to her front door.

"Oh my God, what is wrong with you," screamed Tonya, stumbling through the door for added effect.

Awana raced in behind Tonya, "I should kill you!"

Damn it, my cameras are off in here, thought Tonya as she turned to face Awana.

"You must be ready to square up, running up on me like a crazy person. What's wrong with you?"

"I'm mad," said Awana.

"Okay." Tonya walked pass Awana and closed the front door.

"You had Lawrence arrested."

Tonya allowed herself a brief smile before she turned to face Awana. She stared at her silently.

"How could you? He's Trixie's dad. Say something," yelled Awana as Tonya remained silent.

"He got himself arrested, pervert."

"That's a lie, and you know it. You doctored the footage to make him look bad," said Awana.

"I can't believe how horrible you look. Never let a man bring you this low. Aren't you two getting a divorce? Instead of barging into my home, you should be strategizing with your attorney. His arrest could get you everything."

"Do you always have to win?" asked Awana.

"Of course."

Awana looked around Tonya's living room, "You have every material item a person could want. You're beautiful and educated, yet you still can't let your guard down."

Tonya took a seat on the sofa with a bored look on her face, "How much is this session going to cost me, doctor?"

"Don't you understand how your actions will affect Trixie? How do you think she is going to feel when she finds out you recorded an innocent conversation she had with her friend and used it to have her dad arrested?

"She'll be fine."

"Really, were you fine when your parents divorced, and your dad shut you out his life? Because that's how all of this got started, isn't it? You had to rely on yourself after being a daddy's girl for years. I bet you ran across several men who only looked at you as a pretty face when you were making a name for yourself in your career. Don't you see how different things would have been if your dad had remained an influence in your life? Do you want Trixie caught in the middle of you and Lawrence's drama? She deserves better. You don't have to do this alone anymore."

"Look-" Tonya's doorbell rang. "You in here preaching like you belong. Get the door."

Awana walked to the door, shaking her head. Pastor Donnelly rushed into the room.

"Tonya, I need to speak to you about something important."

"Pastor Donnelly, I thought I explained myself last time. You are getting too involved in my personal business. Awana shouldn't have called you over here. I will consider telling the cops I made a mistake if Lawrence accepts weekly visitation and allows me full custody of Trixie."

Pastor Donnelly sat next to Tonya and grabbed her hands, "I'm not here for that. It's about Trixie."

Tonya jumped up from the sofa in frustration, "Why does everyone think they know what's best for my daughter. You need to leave, both of you."

"Tonya, I need to speak to you before the police get here."

"Police? Why are the police coming here?" asked Awana.

"Be quiet. Why are you still here?"

Awana moved closer to Tonya, "I get it. You're the big bad hood girl turned business mogul, but ain't nobody afraid of you. Inside, you're just a weak little girl longing for her daddy."

Pastor Donnelly moved between Awana and Tonya. He grabbed Tonya by the arms, "Listen to me. Trixie has been taken."

"Taken, what do you mean? Taken where?" Pastor Donnelly pulled out his phone, "Sit down, please. Let me explain."

"Explain what? Just say it," said Awana.

Tonya stared at Pastor Donnelly, her heartbeat drumming loudly in her ears.

"I have a team who does outreach with different sex trafficking organizations."

"Sex trafficking?" asked Awana.

Pastor Donnelly grabbed Tonya's hand, "Tonya? Do you understand what I'm saying? One of the members saw Trixie's picture on a site known for trafficking minors. The police are on the way to interview you."

Tonya took the cell phone from Pastor Donnelly. It was open to a picture of Trixie dressed in lingerie spread across a four-poster bed. She appeared to be sleeping. Her hair was draped across one shoulder. Beneath the photo was the caption: *I fell asleep waiting for you to cum.*

The phone fell from Tonya's hands.

"Lord, Jesus," said Awana picking up the phone.

"Is there anyone you want me to call," asked Pastor Donnelly.

"Momma," said Tonya as she gently traced the picture of Trixie with her fingertip.

EPISODE THIRTEEN

40,300,000: THE INTERNATIONAL LABOR ORGANIZATION

Trixie pulled at her restraints for the hundredth time. Her wrists and ankles were raw. The man in the mask told her she would be punished if she kept pulling the ropes, but she didn't care. She knew they were going to do something terrible to her if they hadn't already. She didn't think she was sore, but she couldn't tell because her legs were spread wide and tethered to the bedposts. The masked man must have dressed her while she was unconscious. She woke up in a lace bralette and see-through underwear. It was freezing in the room. Her body started to shiver.

"Would you like a blanket," said a female voice.

Trixie turned her head as much as she could to find the voice.

"It's a speaker. We're watching you, so I would stop pulling on your ropes. You don't want him to punish you."

"Let me go. My mother has lots of money. She'll pay you."

"What's your name?"

"Trixie."

"I'm Lilly. It doesn't matter how much money you have.

It's about his reputation. The best girls keep his customers coming back."

Trixie looked around the room for clothes. She couldn't tell where she was, but there were bars on the windows and cameras at the top of the walls. The few furnishings in the room appeared expensive.

"What is this place," asked Trixie.

"The Waiting Room. You're lucky Lex likes to pamper his girls. He says it makes them sweeter."

Trixie started pulling on her ropes and screaming, "Let me out! Let me out!"

Lilly rushed into the room, climbed onto the bed, and slapped Trixie. She grabbed her by the shoulders and shook her.

"Shut up. Shut your mouth. Stupid."

"Out."

Lilly scrambled off the bed and rushed to the corner of the room head bowed.

"Lilly, get our guest a blanket, please." Lilly rushed past the masked man to the door.

"Lilly," he called.

Lilly took tentative steps back into the room. She stopped in front of the masked man, stood on her tiptoes, and placed a brief kiss on his lips. He grabbed her by her hair, pulling her almost off the ground. Lilly placed her hands on his cheeks and ground her mouth into his. The kiss lasted several seconds before she scurried out the room.

"No, please," whimpered Trixie as he approached the bed.

"It's ok. I just want to help ease some of your anxiety. Ask me anything. I want you to feel comfortable.

"I want to go home."

"I'm afraid that's not possible. I paid good money for you."

"Lex, please." Lex trailed a finger down the top of Trixie's thigh, "So you know who I am? Good. What else do you want to know?"

"My mom has a lot of money and-"

Lex lay next to Trixie, his head on her shoulder, "I know who you are."

"You do?"

"Of course, I've been watching you for. Would you like to know how?"

Trixie shook her head.

"Your pictures are beautiful. You're a classy girl- rich, educated. You know about the finer things in life, and I like that."

Trixie tried to move Lex's head off her shoulder. He drew patterns on her stomach, making her nervous. She clenched her stomach muscles.

"Relax. I'm not going to take you. I'm going to groom you."

"For what?" asked Trixie.

Lex stood by the side of the bed. "I'm going to be patient with you if you obey me. You will be the companion to my high-profile clients. You will wear the best clothes and ride on private jets to exotic locations. If the money is right, you may go to one owner. I've been thinking about diversifying my interests."

Tears rolled down her cheeks, "No, please. You can't sell me. This isn't right. Let me go!"

Lex walked to the door, "Please, save your voice. My clients like a little conversation first. I will have Lilly bring you newspapers to read."

A few moments later, Lilly entered the room. Her lips were swollen and bleeding slightly from kissing Lex.

***

Tonya lay in bed, curled on her side a tray of food beside her. Her dad was sitting in a chair, staring out the window while her mother attempted to change her nightgown.

"Tonya, please. It's been three days. You won't eat. You haven't spoken to anyone. I'm worried about you. So is your father."

Tonya shifted on her back and stared at the ceiling.

"Pastor Donnelly is coming by later. Do you want him to see you like this?"

Tonya continued ignoring her mother. Theresa slammed the tray of food on the nightstand and stormed out the room.

Tonya's dad closed the bedroom door and went to sit on the edge of the bed. "When you were a baby, you were ugly. You had a little tuft of hair at the top of your head. You were all red, wrinkly, and skinny. Lord knows I didn't want no skinny baby. I used to sneak cereal in your bottle when Theresa wasn't looking until you grew chubby and dimply."

Grant chuckled and shifted on the bed, "The older you got, the more beautiful you grew to be. Not just on the outside but inside too."

Valerie walked into the room, "You were the most generous person. You always shared your lunch and hair bows with the girls at school. You didn't want people to know because you pretended to be tough, but inside, you were soft and sweet like a marshmallow."

Valerie walked towards the vacant side of the bed, squeezing Grant's shoulder. He put his hand on Valerie's and heaved himself off the bed. *Take care of my baby he whispered, exiting.*

Valerie brushed the hair out of Tonya's eyes and squeezed her hand, "You were always giving advice. You swore you knew everything. Never mind the fact you were always right."

Valerie scooted down in the bed and curled up next to Tonya, who smiled slightly.

***

Lilly's stringy hair hung around her face. The clothes on her willowy frame hung loosely. The faded bruise under her eye and the scratches on her hand did nothing to make Trixie feel sorry for her. For the last few days, Lilly had been a nightmare. She shortened Trixie's shower time and brought her cold food. Now Trixie felt tortured. Lex told Lilly to massage and lotion Trixie's skin before her next set of pictures, but Trixie felt as if Lilly was pounding her flesh.

"Stop."

"I'm not done," said Lilly.

"Let's pretend you're done."

Lilly tossed the bottle of lotion on the nightstand, "Fine."

"If you don't want me here, why don't you help me escape?"

Lilly paced the room, pulling out her hair by the strand.

"What are you doing? Stop that."

"You just don't get it do you? You don't understand how good you have it."

"He gon' sell me! What's good about that! I'm better than this."

"So, I deserve this, and you don't?"

Trixie got up on her knees. Her ankles were freed the second day as a reward for good behavior. Now, only one of her hands was bound by a link chain and handcuff.

"I didn't grow up in a poor neighborhood. My mom is rich, and my dad has money too. Stuff like this is not supposed to happen to girls like me."

"Don't act like you're better than me. At least my dad was around."

Trixie was silent for a moment, "How do you know about me?"

Lilly stared at Trixie and thought about her family. Her dad was a good dad. They didn't have much, but he came home every night. He made sure to bring her a treat at least once a week and pat her mom on the butt telling her how beautiful she was even when she was in a crisis. Lilly's mom had a neurological disorder that made her tired all the time. One day, Lilly's dad didn't come home. He died in a car crash. Several months later Lilly's mom had a health crisis and never recovered. Lilly dodged social services for about a year, and then eventually met Lex. He gave her a stable home and three meals a day.

Lilly picked up the lotion and scrubbing brush, "Forget it rich girl. Don't expect dinner tonight."

"Wait, I'll give you ten thousand dollars."

"Sure, have your mom cash app me."

Trixie pulled on the chain and started screaming at the top of her lungs.

"Be quiet. Have you lost it?"

Trixie started making animal-like sounds, biting her arms and pulling out her hair.

"What's wrong with you? Stop! I'll tell you how I know about your dad."

Trixie stared at Lilly breathing hard. She waited for her to speak.

"You think your money makes you better than me, but your money got you into this."

"What are you talking about?"

"That fancy school you go to."

"McDuffie is a magnet school, but it ain't all that," said Trixie rubbing her bruised arms.

"Your counselor recorded your sessions and posted them online. That's where Rico finds his girls."

"Who is Rico?"

Lilly ran to Trixie and grabbed a fistful of her hair, "Forget that name. If you don't, I will kill you. I've done it before."

"You've killed someone before?" asked Trixie rubbing her scalp.

"Around here, loyalty is rewarded. All I need do is go to school and find new girls. I'm not gonna let you get me in trouble."

"You have sex with Lex? I saw you kiss him on the first day. Is he cute under his mask? Maybe I could get next to him, and he wouldn't sell me?"

"You don't have it in you."

"You don't know me," said Trixie.

"They know you are a virgin."

"So."

Lilly started pulling out strands of her hair again. Trixie pulled a few of her own to understand why Lilly did it. "It's best if you do it yourself," said Lilly.

"Do what?"

"Lose your virginity."

"Something's wrong with you. I got to get out of here," said Trixie pulling her chain.

"If the client doesn't want a virgin. I can bring you something to do it before he comes."

Tears rolled down Trixie's face, "Do what before who comes?"

Lilly sat on the bed next to Trixie. "I wasn't a virgin, but some of the other girls were. If you want me to help you, you need to be nicer to me. I can even bring you some pills," said Lilly leaving out the door.

"Pills for what!" yelled Trixie.

"To make you forget," whispered Lilly behind the closed door.

EPISODE FOURTEEN

THE VILLAGE

Tonya's living room was a makeshift assembly line. Vince and the crew had flyers sorted in stacks of twenty-five for the volunteers to plaster around the neighborhood. Pastor Donnelly had twenty volunteers from the church coming, and the parents and youth at the community center were already on the streets.

"Good job, guys," said Pastor Donnelly.

"Is Trixie's mom coming? I heard she was a bad B."

Vince pushed his homie on the shoulder, "Shut up, man. Don't talk about my girl's mom."

Pastor Donnelly put a stack of flyers on the table and walked out of the room.

"What's wrong with him? Everybody acting overprotective of Trixie and her mother," whined Missy.

"Look, if you can't be nice, you can leave. Her mom is sick. Like in a coma or something," said Vince.

"Fa real?" asked Rockelle.

"I heard she stopped talking. Just stays in her room," said Vince.

"That's messed up," said Missy.

Vince hauled a box of flyers to the floor, "That's why you can't be saying crazy stuff about Trixie. I know you don't like her but think about how she feels. Her daughter on some pervert site."

"What kind of site?" asked one of Vince's friends.

"I saw it," said Rockelle. She was in some purple lace stuff all spread open."

"Shut up, Rockelle and don't nobody say nothing else about it or look at the picture," said Vince.

"When I lived in Detroit, a lot of girls would go missing. I heard sex traffickers would sell them and make them prostitute and stuff."

Missy grabbed a stack of flyers and her purse, "I'm gonna head out. I'll take some flyers with me."

Rockelle picked up a stack of flyers following Missy, "Bye, y'all."

Missy fidgeted by the door, "I forgot I had something to do. I'll catch up later."

"Whatever," said Rockelle.

As she exited, Lawrence stormed through the front door. He was clean-shaven and well dressed. Dark circles under his eyes mad him appear mad. He looked as if he had lost weight.

"Tonya! Tonya!" yelled Lawrence. Pastor Donnelly came rushing into the room.

"Please keep it down. She's resting."

"She could be on her death bed, you could be performing last rites, and I wouldn't care. Enough is enough. First, she tried to keep me from my daughter, and then she had me jailed. I came to get answers about my daughter."

"Let's be fair. Tonya wanted to share custody of Trixie with you, but you wanted sole custody instead. A lot of this could have been avoided," said Pastor Donnelly.

"Tonya must have you whipped. I know how she operates."

Pastor Donnelly grabbed Lawrence by the collar while Vince and his friend tried to break up the struggle.

"Stop it right now."

"Mom?" Lawrence shoved Pastor Donnelly and Vince out of the way.

"You two take that mess outside. Tonya does not need to hear the commotion," said Lawrence's mother.

"I thought you were staying at a hotel."

"I am, but I came to sit with Tonya while her mother ran errands. That poor girl."

"She had me arrested. Stole my child."

Vince motioned for his friends to follow him into the kitchen.

"I know you're upset with Tonya, but we have to think about Trixie. How do you think she will be affected when she comes home to find her mother a zombie?"

Lawrence went to pass his mother to get to Tonya's room, but she stopped him.

"I need to see her for myself. You don't know her like I do. She's a good actress."

"She hasn't eaten in three days. The doctor had to give her medicine to sleep. It's like her body shut down. She can hear us, but she's out of it."

"Why isn't she in a hospital?"

"Her momma feels she needs to stay here until Trixie returns."

Pastor Donnelly extended his arm to shake Lawrence's hand, "Truce?"

"We are all on the same team. Pastor Donnelly has a team of people looking for Trixie. He's been on the news and radio," said Lawrence's mother.

"We good," said Lawrence ignoring Pastor Donnelly's hand.

***

Missy rummaged through her stepfather's clothes in his drawer. She swiped her hand under the edge of the dresser and behind the paintings on the wall. She was looking for anything to support her suspicions. Walking into the closet, she checked the pockets of his jeans and his jackets. Along the wall were rows of shoeboxes. She quickly went through several boxes, knowing her time was limited. She found it, his second cell phone. She powered on the phone glad it was a basic Trac phone with a pin code. She entered her mother's birthday, his birthday, and 6969. None of those worked. She sat down on the floor for a moment. When Vince said Trixie's picture was on a trafficking site, she knew it was her stepfather. She just needed to prove it. She picked up the phone and entered her birthday, bingo.

"Grimy bastard." Missy went through his pictures first. There were dozens of pictures of young girls. Some taken at a distance other were selfies, but no pictures of Trixie. She checked his text messages next. Most of his texts were pictures he sent to the same number. His last few texts were pictures of him and Trixie lying in his bed. Missy instantly sent herself a screenshot of the number he texted and deleted the file. She also deleted the pictures of Trixie and straightened up the closet.

"Hey."

Missy jumped and turned around to face her stepfather. "I was just looking for something to wear. I was tired of wearing my old stuff."

"Why don't you try it on? Let me see how it looks."

"I didn't find anything," said Missy sliding past her stepfather.

He grabbed her by the hand, pulled her closer. "I haven't seen you in a while. You mad at me?"

"Just busy."

"Well, you need to be busy around here too. It's not fair to let your momma do all the work."

"Ok, I will clean up the house and wash all the clothes. I know y'all be tired from working."

"That'll be a big help." Missy rushed to the bedroom door.

"Missy," called her stepfather, following her to the door. She paused.

"You been neglecting some things in here too. You take care of those first. I wouldn't want you to be too tired after cleaning the house," he said and closed the bedroom door pulling her inside.

EPISODE FIFTEEN

GILDED CAGE

One, two, three… one, two, three, on and on. Trixie twirled to the music in the arms of Lex's bodyguard, a slim, wiry Asian man. Trixie asked Lilly how he could protect anyone, but Lilly told her he was quick with a blade. Trixie tried to stifle a yawn as she turned the ballroom again. Her feet and back ached, but she didn't complain. Instead, she relished the time away from her room and secretly eyeballed the layout of the home whenever she had the opportunity. There had to be other girls in the house because occasionally she heard raised voices. Lilly told her there would be a big party tonight, and she would play the host. Normally, Trixie saw her throughout the day, but she laughingly told her that she would be getting primped for the party. Finally, the music ended. As Trixie turned to leave, her dance partner pinched her butt. Trixie turned around ready to fight.

"Just warming you up for tonight. No harm, pretty girl."

"Trixie let's go. We have a lot to do," called Lilly from the doorway.

Trixie followed Lilly down the hall, "I thought you were going to spend all day at the spa?"

"Ssh," Lilly pushed Trixie into the room and shoved her against the wall.

"Move." Trixie attempted to push Lilly out of her face.

"He's going to sell me."

Trixie stared at Lilly, Huh? But I thought you said- I don't get it."

Lilly walked towards the bed with tears in her eyes.

"I heard the guards talking about me. He promised he would be the only one," whispered Lilly.

"Is he gonna sell me too?" asked Trixie.

"You were sold before you got here. You think your mom would give me money to disappear?"

"She has lots of money. I promise. My dad will help too." Trixie hopped off the bed and paced the room, "We have to get out of here," said Trixie.

Lilly walked to the door, aware of the cameras in the room. She hoped no one would view the footage, but if so, maybe it would be without sound.

"Be ready for six. Wear the purple dress with nothing underneath," yelled Lilly.

Trixie stood on the other side of the room arms folded across her body.

"I have a plan," mumbled Lilly before she left.

***

The ballroom shined in brilliant shades of purple, gold and green. Spotlights circled the dark room, making it impossible to see the masked faces. Classical music filtered between the guests as the band played in the left corner. To the right of the band was a DJ table. After several hours of polite chit chat, the party turned rowdy, and sex flowed freely. Dozens of girls entertained male guests of all shapes and sizes from different nationalities. Most of them were there by choice. However, several girls had been in Trixie's position years before they were auctioned to high-paying customers and their wives. A few of the girls currently worked the Cantinas, servicing up to thirty men a night. Most of them were rough around the edges and were brought in to service the guests who had fetishes and violent tendencies.

Trixie entered the room behind her bodyguards. Her dress was a flowing ball gown, high in the front and cut right above her butt in the back. Jewelry adorned her neck, ears and wrists. Her hair was in a high ponytail. Alicia had given her a facial until her skin glowed. The only makeup she wore was a clear gloss.

Trixie trailed closely behind her bodyguards as they pressed through hordes of people. She contemplated trying to escape, but her thoughts were not clear. Lex made his way to Trixie. He had the look of a polished businessman in his tuxedo and bowtie.

"Wh-where's your mask," Trixie slurred. "You not afraid, I see you? Youuu punk."

"This is my party. I want my guests to feel safe here." Lex leaned closer, "Besides, this is goodbye, pretty girl."

Lex's bodyguard pulled him to the side, "You want me to give her some more?"

Lex grabbed a glass of champagne from a passing waiter, "Just a few drops. She needs to be awake for her wedding night."

Both men chuckled and pounded fists as Trixie was swept away to dance with one of the guests.

EPISODE SIXTEEN

DADDY SYNDROME

Tonya lay in bed, stared at the ceiling. She knew her family was disappointed she hadn't responded to them, but she was not ready to accept that Trixie was in a dingy basement having numerous unknown men assault her. While everyone talked over her and her mother brushed her hair, she imagined Trixie starving or laying in an alley beaten. If she woke up, she would have to accept that Valerie was right. She needed professional help. If she got out of bed, she would have to watch her parents blame themselves for how they raised her. Most importantly, she couldn't face the embarrassment of Lawrence knowing she wasn't the better parent after all. She knew Trixie need her, expected her to crush mountains to save her. Well, there wouldn't be any mountain crushing today, but soon.

***

Lilly adjusted the straps of her gown and walked into the ballroom. She was angry and felt betrayed. How could she drop her guard and believe Lex thought she was good enough to take care of him and the girls exclusively. She should have known he was toying with her. All the years she lived with him, the only women he put in charge were beautiful and glamourous, not skinny and small chested. They knew how to speak and mingle with his wealthy guests. He chose girls like Trixie. Lilly may not be the ideal beauty, but she was smart. She would get her and Trixie away from him then she would make sure he regretted looking down on her. Will, one of the workers she befriended would help them escape. He had been with Lex most of his life. His father was the cook and a childhood friend of Lex. Lex always hired relatives or friends from childhood. Unlike most employers, he treated his people well. He didn't talk down to them or lord his wealth over them like an invincible God.

To them, it was like any other job. It paid well, and they lived a hundred times better than they would on their own. Will, however, wanted more. For years, tried to convince his father to let him join the military or go to college to be a lawyer. However, his father owed a lot to Lex. His contract was for life, which included his children.

The deciding moment for Will came when he overheard his father telling a friend that he was afraid Will would have to do illegal work for Lex if he became a lawyer or got specialized military skill. Will was enraged. For years, his father made it seem as if he and Lex were best friends, but the balance of power was clear. Lex wasn't even the person in charge. Some man named Rico was. He held all the cards and expected everyone to fall in line. When he confronted his father, his dad made it clear that if anything happened to Lex, they were still bound to Rico. The only thing that made sense to Will was to be the next person in charge. Because that would never happen, he decided to get his father away from Lex and the business.

"Walk straight," Will whispered to Lilly as he passed her a glass of champagne.

"Let your girl know she needs to throw up on the man in the red jacket. He's the one who bought her. He will want the doctor to look her over before he gives Lex the final payment," said Will.

"You don't have to tell me again. I got it," Lilly replied.

"Are you serving or trying to get some cat?" asked one of the bodyguards, walking up to Will and Lilly.

Will walked off to serve the rest of the guests, and Lilly went to find Trixie.

"Trixie get up. You have to mingle with the rest of the guest until your owner comes." Trixie attempted to stand straight but slumped back against the wall.

"Take your shoes off. You can't mess this up because you can't walk in heels. You see the guy in the red jacket? In about three minutes, go stand by him and flirt. You have to stay close to him for the plan to work."

Lilly dropped a pill in Trixie's glass of champagne, "Drink this. It will make you sick, but you will be ok. We have to get Lex to call the doctor for you."

Trixie tried to explain to Lilly she'd already been drugged, but her nausea and lightheadedness had tripled.

"Go." Lilly shoved the glass to Trixie's lips, forcing the liquid down her throat then shoved her in the direction of the bar and left to find Will.

"All set?" asked Will.

"I gave her the pill and told her to stay close to him. I didn't want to share anything else in case she started talking."

Will pulled Lilly down the hall, "When you get about thirty minutes away, dump Trixie out the car."

"But I need her. Her mom is going to give me money for saving her."

"Do you believe that? Once her parents have their

precious daughter back they will call the cops. If you are not arrested, you will have to snitch on everybody."

"I will take my chances with Lex."

Will pushed Lilly against the wall. "Are you serious? You'd rather be treated like a blow-up doll laying with different men every night?"

"I don't have a family. This is all I have."

Will ran his fingers through his hair. He wished he had never involved Lilly. He was scared she was brainwashed. "Look, if you want out, stay out. If you come back, I will kill you. I can't have you jeopardizing my father's life."

Lilly pushed Will out of the way and turned to go, "I will get Trixie away from here. Then I'm gonna rob her people and go far away."

Will swore softly. He wasn't a killer, but he did want to survive. "I will put some money in the jeep for you. Dump Trixie then call the cops with the phone I left inside. She'll be okay."

"How much money are you giving me?"

"Just stick to the plan. I got you. Take the keys to the jeep." Lilly took the keys and turned to head back into the party.

"Hey, don't you care if I make it out safely?" joked Will. Lilly gave him the middle finger and kept walking.

Trixie turned away from the bar and vomited on the man in the red jacket's hand and shiny black shoes. Lilly walked over to the bar to make sure someone called the doctor when Trixie fell to the floor. She started seizing and foaming at the mouth. Ahead of her, Lilly saw Lex and his bodyguard rush towards Trixie. Alarmed, she turned and fled. She hoped Will put the money in the jeep. If not, she would find Tonya's house and sell Trixie's location. Lilly turned to look at Trixie one more time when the doors to the ballroom burst open. Dozens of cops swarmed into the room. She turned and fled in the opposite direction. A few feet away, she slipped into an unoccupied room. She searched the room for something to break the window when Lex and one of his bodyguards entered and rushed into the closet. Lilly looked in the closet where a secret door opened.

I don't need him, she thought and turned to exit the room, but Lex dragged her back into the closet.

"Let's go. Don't you know they will take you away from me?"

Lilly struggled as he dragged her into another part of the house. In a burst of energy, she pulled away from him. The front of her dressed ripped. Lilly stared in horror as the key to the jeep tumbled to the floor. She stared into Lex's blank eyes.

He knows, she thought as her world went black.

EPISODE SEVENTEEN

WHOLENESS

T he smell of antiseptic was first. The pain was next.
"Am I still a virgin?" mumbled Trixie.

"You better be. You supposed to be saving that for me."

Trixie opened her eyes and glanced around the room.
Vince's face, fixed in a silly grin, hovered over her. She tested
her voice, but no sound emerged.

"I heard the doctor talking to your dad. She said no one
touched you. Awana made an appointment for you to see a
shrink, so get ready. Man, I'm gonna miss your grandma's
cooking. She's been burning up the kitchen."

Trixie attempted to raise her head, moaning in pain.

"Ssh, I snuck in here. Your other grandmother talked
your dad into taking a walk. They gonna be back in a little."

"You ok?" squeaked Trixie.

"I'm straight. The whole crew has been looking for you.
Look, they made a video."

Vince pulled out his cell phone. The faces of his crew
filled the scene. They clowned around and told her to get
well. A couple of guys joked about wanting to see more of
the dance moves she was doing at the party.

"Oh," managed Trixie.

Vince chuckled, "They are just being silly."

"I didn't see Missy on the video."

Vince paused for a moment, swallowed, "Don't worry about her. Just get better so you can go home. I don't want to keep sneaking in here to see you."

Trixie struggled to sit up in the bed, "Where's my mom?"

"Lie back down and wait until your dad gets here."

"Where is my mom?" asked Trixie again.

"At home."

Trixie tried to get out of the bed, "What's wrong with her."

Vince grabbed Trixie by the shoulders, attempting to push her back onto the bed.

"Get off me. She should be here. I need to find her."

"You're gonna hurt yourself," said Vince.

Trixie pounded Vince on the chest. I know something is wrong. I know it."

Lawrence and his mother rushed into the room, "What are you doing to her?" he asked.

Vince pulled away from Trixie, "She's trying to go see her mom."

"What's wrong with my mom?"

"Sweetheart, please calm down," said Lawrence's mother.

Lawrence sat on the bed next to Trixie and put his arms around her, "Your mom can't be here right now."

"Why not? I don't understand."

Lawrence's mother approached the bed and placed her hand on Trixie's leg.

"Tell her," said Vince.

"Get out of here," Lawrence replied.

"I'm gonna leave and find her if you don't tell me."

"She's in a coma," blurted Vince.

Lawrence held Trixie tighter as she sobbed, "That's not true, baby. She's not unconscious. She's just not talking right now. She got scared when she found out what happened to you."

"Well, let's go. She'll be better because I'm home now." Lawrence's mother walked out the room to get the nurse.

"Honey, I will leave and tell her we've found you safe, however, you've got to stay here for a few days. We need to make sure you're ok."

"I'm fine. No one did anything to me. They gave me drugs. That's all."

"The doctors want to monitor you to make sure you're going to be fine."

"Dad?"

Lawrence held his breath, "Yes."

Trixie pulled away and lay on her side, "I will never stay here when my mom needs me."

Vince motioned for Lawrence to meet him outside.

"If the doctor's say she's ok, you need to take her home, said Vince.

"I know. She's stubborn like her mom. The minute I blink, she will be gone."

"She asked about Missy," said Vince.

"Did you tell her?"

"Nah," said Vince shaking his head and walking away.

***

Theresa and Lawrence's mom finished the last of the cleaning while Grant and Lawrence's dad grilled in the back yard. Neither one of them said the food might go to waste because they needed something to do. Maybe if Trixie was up to it, she might want to have a few friends over to take keep her from worrying about her mother. Despite Trixie's best attempts, the doctors held her in the hospital another three days. Lawrence and Awana were bringing her home today.

"I sure hope the peace holds," said Lawrence's dad.

"I wish I had faith that Tonya will do the right thing, but she didn't speak to her mother and me for almost twenty years."

"Damn."

"She kept in touch with us through Valerie. Although she never admitted it, she needed to hear how we were doing."

"Whatcha think about Tonya and the preacher?"

"He's crazy. My daughter will eat him up."

"I'm sure he won't mind."

Trixie walked into the front door and rushed towards her mother's room. Valerie and Theresa intercepted her.

"Hey, baby," said Theresa. "You're looking much better."

"Thank you."

Valerie grabbed Trixie in a big hug, "I was so worried about you."

"I'm ok. I just need to see my momma."

Theresa and Valerie glanced at each other, "We told Tonya you were safe, but... but, she still hasn't got better. I just want to prepare you, okay?" said Theresa.

Wordlessly, Trixie walked around Valerie and Theresa into her mother's room. "Momma? It's me. I'm home."

Trixie stood over the bed and looked down at Tonya. She was pale and had lost several pounds. There was an IV in her arm attached to a monitor.

"That's to give her fluids," Awana said from the doorway.

"Is she dead?"

"Of course not. Sometimes she opens her eyes and eats a bit of food. Talk to her."

"Hey, momma. Are you ok? Momma!" Trixie felt a

strong arm across her shoulders. Lawrence squeezed her softly.

"Do you want us to leave the two of you alone? You have about an hour before the nurse arrives."

"You don't have to be here by yourself if you don't want to. I can sit with you," said Awana.

"We will make sure she's taken care of. Thanks for going with me to pick her up from the hospital," said Lawrence turning away from Awana.

Dismissed, Awana made her way down the hall towards the front door.

"Are you coming back later?" asked Valerie.

Awana snorted, "Not likely. You heard him."

"This is not his house. Trixie wants you here."

"It's too hard. We're divorcing, and I need to get used to not having him around."

Valerie gestured for Awana to sit next to her on the sofa.

"I'm divorcing my husband too. He cheated with some Paleo dieting muscle chick. I tried to hold on to him, make him love me, but he doesn't. Not anymore. I saw it in his eyes. Lawrence's eyes may say a lot of things, but 'it's over' is not one of them."

Awana put her head in her hands, "He wants children. I'm barren."

"You may not be able to produce children, but you're far from barren. How many lives do you touch at the center every day? Lawrence is a grown man, and he will be alright. It's not his body. If he doesn't want to adopt or foster, too bad. Do it on your own."

Valerie took a deep breath, "Sorry. I'm working on being more assertive. Tonya used to rag on me all the time about being too quiet. She was right. She was right about my husband too."

"It's ok. I know you're telling the truth. It's just gonna take getting used to."

"Will you be here when Vince tells her about Missy?"

"I don't think he should."

"Professionally, I agree. But what if she finds out online. Plus, maybe going to the funeral will be healing."

Awana and Valerie sat quietly, each thinking of Missy. How she died. How Trixie lived. When the police raided the house where Trixie was held, Chris went into a panic. He confronted Missy about the pictures missing from his phone, and she confessed to sending the information to the cops along with the girls he helped Lex find. He killed Missy and himself before the cops arrived. Missy's mother discovered their bodies.

In the room, Trixie and Theresa attempted to make Tonya more comfortable on the bed.

"I got it, grandma."

"We can do it together. Sometimes her body feels like dead weight."

"I can do it. Please," said Trixie wringing the excess water from the bath towel.

Theresa left the room, and Trixie finished disrobing her mother. She grabbed her mother's favorite body wash and squeezed some into the pan of water by Tonya's bedside. After bathing Tonya and smoothing her skin with her favorite lotion, Trixie threw the house clothes her grandmother bought for Tonya in the trash.

"You see that momma, cotton pajamas. Grandma tripping."

Trixie went into her mother's closet and pulled out one of her lingerie sets. She struggled, but she managed to dress her mother.

"I'm gonna oil your scalp so your hair doesn't dry out. I

hope they've been putting cocoa butter on your hands and feet. Your lips look a little ashy."

Trixie waited to see if her mother would respond, "I'm going to get our hairdresser to whip up a dry shampoo for you. Then I'm gonna get you something to eat from your favorite restaurant."

Trixie climbed into the bed and placed Tonya between her legs, "No offense to grandma, but you've probably been eating too many fat backs. We not used to that, huh mama? We eat the best."

Trixie waited for her mother to respond, "Don't worry, momma. I got us," said Trixie as she parted her mother's scalp lining each row with coconut oil. Tearfully, she grabbed the remote control and turned on the television.

"Can I be Jackee this time?"